The
SEEKER

The SEEKER

Robert Barlow Fox

SANTA FE

This is a work of fiction. Names, characters, places and incidents either are the product of the author's imagination or are used fictitiously, and any resemblance to any actual persons, living or dead, events, or locales is entirely coincidental.

Sunstone books may be purchased for educational, business, or sales promotional use. For information please write: Special Markets Department, Sunstone Press, P.O. Box 2321, Santa Fe, New Mexico 87504-2321.

—————————————————————————

Library of Congress Cataloging-in-Publication Data:
Fox, Robert B. (Robert Barlow), 1930–
 The seeker / Robert Barlow Fox.
  p. cm.
ISBN: 0-86534-487-6 (pbk. : alk. paper)
1. Survival after airplane accidents, shipwrecks, etc.—Fiction.
2. Teenage boys—Fiction. 3. Amnesia—Fiction. 4. Identity (Psychology)—Fiction.
5. Psychological fiction. I. Title.

PS3556.O947S44 2006
813'.54—dc22

                                        2005057490

—————————————————————————

WWW.SUNSTONEPRESS.COM
SUNSTONE PRESS / POST OFFICE BOX 2321 / SANTA FE, NM 87504-2321 /USA
(505) 988-4418 / ORDERS ONLY (800) 243-5644 / FAX (505) 988-1025

DEDICATION

TO SEEKERS WHO FOLLOW THEIR DREAM
AND MAKE IT A REALITY.

"WHAEA I TE ITI KAHURANGI KI TE TUOHU
KOE MA TE MAUNGA TEI TEI."

SEEK AFTER THE DESIRE OF YOUR HEART. IF YOU
BOW YOUR HEAD LET IT BE TO A LOFTY MOUNTAIN.
—MAORI PROVERB—

PART ONE

Instruction

News Item:

Flight 349 from Los Angeles to Chicago crashed in a violent Thunderstorm in the Rocky Mountains about one hundred miles out of Denver. Search and rescue crew struggled through rugged terrain to reach the crash site at noon on Thursday. Wreckage was scattered over a two mile area. There were no survivors among the hundred and twenty Passengers and eight crew members. But there was ONE survivor known to none...Not even to The survivor.

CHAPTER ONE

Sunshine awakened the boy. He lay quietly enjoying the peacefulness. Suddenly, he came wide awake, eyelids fluttering open, revealing terror-filled brown eyes, his short mahogany hair disheveled on top. He started to sit up. Ooohhhh," he cried in alarm as he grabbed a tree limb. He had almost fallen. He was resting precariously on the branch of a tall pine tree, thirty feet above the ground. "What? Where am I?" He looked around in alarm and confusion. "How did I get here? Way up in a tree?"

His white shirt and blue slacks were damp, but drying in the sun. His left shirt sleeve torn slightly near the elbow. His left eye was swollen in his tan face and he felt stiff and sore, but otherwise okay. Cautiously, the dark haired thirteen year old moved to climb down from his dizzying height. Then he stopped to survey the view from his perch. Towering, purple mountains rose in the distance, the air fresh from recent rain. Far off and down a ravine, over the next ridge, he saw smoke curling upward, probably from a campfire or cabin.

"What has happened to me?" he asked of the sky and sun as he gazed upward. "Why am I here?" He resumed his descent and finally reached the ground with relief. But suddenly, he asked the greatest question of all: "Who am I? I don't know my name, who I am, or nothing. I don't remember anything about me. Why is this happening to me?"

No answers came. Only panic. Then loneliness. He sat down on the ground. Tears flowed from his eyes and ran down his cheeks. He didn't bother to wipe them away. He didn't care.

After awhile, he stopped sobbing, and decided, "This doesn't help me with my problem, sitting here crying, doing nothing."

Instinctively, he reached in his pants pockets. In the right, he pulled out a pocketknife with many blades and a beautiful silver pocket watch, like old men once carried. On the back was engraved, "To my loving grandson." From his left pocket he withdrew a wad of money. "Wow! Golleee. I'm rich. But what good is it to me way up here in the mountains?"

He counted it, then muttered, without concern, "Two hundred and seventy eight dollars." He folded it and stuffed it back in his pocket. He searched his rear pockets and found only a handkerchief and comb. But something in his shirt pocket drew his attention. He pulled out a small book with a fine leather cover. "The Holy Bible," he read. He looked inside the cover. In blue ink, a hand written inscription. "Happy twelfth birthday, Jared. From Mom and Dad."

"So my name is Jared and I am twelve years old. Maybe thirteen or fourteen. I don't know how long I have had it. Looks pretty new. At least I'll have something to read."

He opened the Bible. His eyes were drawn to Luke, Chapter Eleven, Verse nine. "Ask and it shall be given you; seek and ye shall find; knock, and the door shall be opened unto you."

He read aloud, "Seek and ye shall find. Find what?" he wondered. "Maybe myself. Who I used to be. Perhaps find who I am now. Two different people. Or maybe someone between. Maybe I can find many new things I never thought about. Maybe I can find out what it all means The whole thing." He paused. "And maybe I can't. But what have I got to lose? It's worth a try.

"I will seek. I will seek and see what I can find. I will be THE SEEKER. JARED THE SEEKER. That's what I'll be."

He felt lightheaded and lighthearted. A weight lifted from him, physically and mentally. He had made a decision. "First, I will need food. Maybe that smoke off in the distance means a cabin. People. Worth a try."

He took out the pocket watch. Three twenty five. Bet I could have guessed by the sun. I'll try it next time. Learn to know the time by the sun. If I start now I can reach the smoke before dark, if I'm lucky. Be kind of scary in the mountains alone at night.

He looked around, gazed out beyond. Pine trees. Quaking Aspens. Great mountains as far as he could see. Beautiful. It was a beautiful world. Did his other self know how beautiful it was? He stood up and started walking. Jared the Seeker had begun his search. What would he find ahead?

CHAPTER TWO

The sun was lowering in the west. The smoke from the cabin seemed to move farther away the longer he walked. His arm throbbed and his eye was nearly swollen shut. He was tired, thirsty, and hungry. His earlier resolution now faced hard reality. He was a lost, bewildered boy in vast, unknown mountains.

"No!" he shouted. "I have christened myself Jared the Seeker. And so I shall be. I will always seek and somehow, sometime, somewhere I will find who I am, why I am, what I am, and what I am supposed to do."

Darkness came early in the forest. Tall trees nearly blotted out the sky. He thought he still knew the direction to the smoke, but he needed rest. He sat on a log and leaned back against a tree, eyes closed.

Suddenly, he awakened. How long had he dozed? Terror. His hair stood at attention. Something was flying out of the sky straight at him. An apparition. A ghost in the air; an undulating, winged shadow in the pale moonlight, racing toward him. He opened his mouth to scream. Nothing came out. He was breathless. The ghost lit on a limb above him and folded its wings. It was a large, majestic owl of more than two feet tall and brown and white speckled. "Who? Who?

"Jared. I am Jared the Seeker," replied the boy, still shaking.

"No, no, I know who you are. I was just giving my night call to the world. By the way, I am Great Horned Owl."

"You scared me near out of my wits, Great Horned Owl."

"Sorry about that, Seeker," the Owl said, his wise, staring, golden eyes glaring down at the boy, "but I couldn't let you sleep the night through. You have things to do, a way to go yet, a destiny to fulfill." Owl stretched his spotted wings lazily.

"How can you speak my language?"

"I am talking to your mind, not aloud. When I speak to creatures in this manner, I am understood in any language. Now let's quit the chatter. Get your rear end up and follow me." Owl spread his enormous wings and sailed silently into the moon-filled night. Jared hurriedly made his legs move and followed, stumbling over rocks and bushes in an attempt to keep up.

Over the next ridge, he saw a cabin far below with a light shining dimly through a single window and smoke curling lazily from the chimney. He was elated. Owl had disappeared. The boy wondered if he had dreamed the great bird.

Bolder than he felt, he rapped on the wooden cabin door. It opened a crack and a blue-white eye, wide with wise question appeared. "Come in, Seeker," rasped a gravelly voice. "I have been expecting you."

The door opened wide, revealing a shriveled, stooped, ancient man, with one eye, the other covered by a black patch, like a pirate, under bushy, white eyebrows. He wore an odd, felt hat with narrow brim, the crown pulled to a point, over wild, white hair that shot out beneath in every direction, his gray beard reaching halfway to the floor, under a long, narrow, crooked nose. He was dressed in a tan shirt, open at his wrinkled neck, under a shaggy coat, with brown pants that had long ago forgotten their creases. He reminded Jared of a hairy gnome from childhood fairy tales.

The boy glanced around nervously. A kerosene lantern sat on a small, wooden, three-legged table, lighting the room in a pleasant glow. A cupboard with no doors hung on the far wall, lined with jars of what appeared to be nuts, herbs, and dried berries. A rustic bed made of rough poles and covered with a tattered, natty quilt that had long ago lost its colors, sat in one corner. A fire burned in a rock fireplace and within an iron pot hung over licking flames, casting off the good smell of stew.

"How do you know me and how could you be expecting me?"

asked Jared hesitantly, stepping in the door, which slowly closed behind him.

"My messengers informed me. You are a Seeker. It is my business to know all Seekers in the area."

"What messengers?" Jared leaned his back tiredly against the closed door.

"None of your business," the old man answered, disgruntled. "But since I know you, I can introduce myself. I am Elijah. I am a prophet. The few humans who know I exist think I am crazy."

"Are you crazy?" blurted Jared, somewhat fearful. It crossed his mind that he should flee, but where could he go?

"What do you think?" asked the strange little man, examining Jared's face with his one eye and raising a bushy eyebrow.

"I...I don't know."

"Course you don't know. You're just a kid. How could you know much of anything. Well, since you are a Seeker, I'll tell you my opinion, not that you deserve it. Crazy is often different. Folks generally don't like people who are different from what they are used to. Now, Seeker, so you have other names. What is it you seek?"

"Jared is my real name. Right now, Mister Elijah, it is food I seek. I'm real hungry. If you could give me something to eat and drink I would pay you well. I have plenty of money."

"Your first mistake, boy. Letting strangers know you have money. If I was the evil, unscrupulous type I might hit you on the head, tie you up, and take all your cash. But you're lucky. I happen to be a nice guy and a prophet besides. Anyway what would I do with money? No use for it here. I fish. I trap. I have nuts, berries, and other goodies galore. Yep, I live off the good earth and give it my humble thanks."

"Don't you get lonely by yourself?"

"Nope. I chose this way. Nice and peaceful. Don't need friends. Have my dog over there. If I was a bad sort I could have sicked him on you and he would have eaten you alive."

Jared had not noticed the dog, obviously a cross between a

Golden Retriever and one of more other breeds. Dog rolled his brown eyes in boredom and went back to sleep under the table.

"What's your dog's name?" Jared inquired.

"Dog, that IS his name. Dog. See how he perks up his floppy ears. He knows we are talking about him.

"Mister Elijah…"

"Drop the mister," the old man said grumpily. "Although I am a prophet, you can call me Elijah."

"Okay, Elijah. I'll be your friend, if you will feed me," Jared bargained.

"Your second mistake, Jared my boy. You should never think you can buy friends. Not with money, food, love, or whatever. Real friends are not for sale; they cannot be bought. Friends just are. Now pull up that box to the table. I have just two boxes; two chairs. Never have used the second one before. Make yourself at home. You are now my guest. I will give you a meal fit for a king, or a prophet, and his guest. Move out of the way, Dog, and let the Seeker sit up to our table." Elijah gave the large dog a friendly shove with his sandalled foot. Dog moved reluctantly to a pile of rags near a far wall and plopped down, waiting patiently for leftovers.

CHAPTER THREE

The steaming concoction placed before him in a large wooden bowl looked like a combination of oatmeal, corn flakes, and chopsuey, but smelled like a favorite stew from…from where? His past? What was his past? Who was he? Who, why, where, what, how? Lots of questions. No answers. "Smells great!" Jared exclaimed.

"Tastes even better than it smells," replied his host.

"What is it? I mean, what's in it?"

"Oh, local weeds and roots. A little bark, nuts, seeds, berries. Wild this and that. Recipe is in my head. Very secret," the old man added, grinning.

The boy hungrily devoured it. Delicious. The old man filled Jared's bowl again. The boy had not fully realized how hungry he was. He couldn't remember, of course, when he had last eaten. "I mean really, don't you get lonely up here in the mountains by yourself?" ask Jared, wiping his mouth with the back of his hand.

The old man settled on the other box at the table. "Nope. Told you I don't. I got Dog here to talk with. Got the birds and animals and wind and stars, sun. All keep me company. Got my reading material on the shelf there. What more do I need?"

Jared looked behind him at a small shelf he hadn't noticed. "What kind of reading material?" he asked.

The old man rested his chin on his hands as he spoke. "Got the holy book, a Bible, just like the little one in your shirt pocket. And there's Will Shakespeare's complete works. And for entertainment, I have a Captain Marvel comic book."

"A comic book?"

"I told you, boy. It's my entertainment. I like when he goes SHAZAM! and it shows a flash of lightning. Then he takes after evil forces. Everything in the world is evil against good and good against evil. Besides, it's an original first issue of Captain Marvel. Worth a million dollars to the right buyer, if I cared to sell it and if I cared for money, which I don't. If I did, I would knock you on your inquisitive head and steal the two hundred and seventy eight dollars right out of your pocket. And don't ask how I know it's there and how much."

"You're no bigger than I am. I might whip you," Jared replied, smiling.

"Nope. You couldn't do it." The old man leaned back, his one blue-white eye squinting wisely, daringly, down his long nose at Jared. "Old age and treachery can whip youth every time."

The boy gave that some thought. "How come you know I have a Bible in my pocket? And how did you know how much money I have?"

"Determined to ask, aren't you?" The old man clucked and cackled like a chicken. Jared guessed that was his form of laughter. It almost made him laugh, but he figured that would not be polite.

When the wise old codger finished cackling, he fixed his eye on the boy with an intense stare. "You don't listen too well, Seeker. I told you I am Elijah the Prophet. You'd better read that little book in your pocket. I am the one that came to turn the hearts of the children to the fathers and the hearts of the fathers to the children. Isn't your heart turned to your father? Don't you want to know who he is?" Elijah inquired.

"Of course I do. I just finished telling you my story. I don't remember who I am. That's why I became a Seeker. The main thing I am seeking is my parents, and to discover who I am… or used to be anyway." The boy dropped his head to stare sadly at the rustic old, wooden floor, worn smooth from ages of unknown feet.

They were quiet for a long time, listening to the crackle of the fire. Finally, Elijah rose and tossed another log on the flames. A shower of blue and orange sparks sprayed upward. He brought an iron pitcher from a dark, cold corner of the cabin, poured a liquid into a tin cup and set it before Jared. "Drink that and wash down your meal. It is called nectar of the gods."

Jared drank eagerly, then smacked his lips. Tastes like fresh berry juice of some kind."

"Blackberries. Grow right in the back yard." The old man moistened his lips, took out a red handkerchief, blew his nose, then raised his one eye as though pondering whether or not to say something. Then he made his decision. "Jared the Seeker," he said softly, "I know who you are. I know why you woke up in that pine tree."

"If you know, why haven't you told me? Why? Why all this talk and waste of time? If you are a prophet, then tell me what you know! I'm beginning to think you're just a crazy old man, like you said those people down in the valley think you are," Jared stated angrily, eyes tearing, then spilling with frustration. The boy let it all out while the old man sat in silence. Dog whined pitifully, empathizing with the young visitor. After awhile, the boy had cried himself out. "How do you know so much and why won't you tell me?"

First, I must tell you it is not easy being a prophet. Logically, I knew you had been in a pine tree because your back is covered with pine needles and pine gum. Wonderful smell, pine. I know who you are from the signs of the rainbow after a storm. And my messengers told me..."

"Who are these messengers? Your imagination?" Jared demanded, cheeks shiny from drying tears.

"None of your business. Well, it might be your business, since you have become The Seeker. So, I'll tell you that one of my messengers is the owl. Didn't he direct you here?"

Jared was amazed. He had not dreamed the great bird after all. He looked at this strange little man through new eyes. "Well...er...yes. That is rather a strange thing I experienced."

"Now, my boy, Jared the Seeker, I cannot reveal the answers to your questions because things happen for a reason, and in your case you were meant to be a seeker. You will experience two lives.

The one you used to live and the person you are now. You are privileged. You will learn things that most people never have a chance to realize.

"Do you think that I am the same person I was at six or twenty, or in my sixties or seventies? A question to think about: Do you think you would know yourself if your present self met yourself at thirty years old coming down the street? You see, we are never the same person from one moment to the next. Just like a river is never the same from one moment to the next. Always moving. Always changing. Wonderful, don't you think?" The old man smiled, revealing ancient, yellowed teeth.

Jared grinned, eyes still a bit blurry from tears. "I am sorry, Elijah, for blowing my cool and saying nasty things to you. By the way," he ventured, "how old are you?"

"None of your business. What would you say if I told you I am three thousand years old?"

"I'd say you're really weird and possibly crazy."

Elijah the Prophet cackled.

"Weren't you ever married. Or didn't you ever want a woman…you know…to be with a woman?" Jared asked boldly.

"At one time, I had that desire. Long ago, very long ago. But the women in the cities want a man who is tall, handsome, sparkling personality, maybe athletic, and wealthy. I just didn't fit the mold in any of those categories.

"Now enough chatter for one sitting. You will stay with me until you get your bearings, then continue on with your seeking. You can have that old bed in the corner. It's softer than it looks. I'll curl up with Dog and my bedroll I use while exploring. We'll talk more tomorrow"

CHAPTER FOUR

The boy, who had christened himself Jared the Seeker, had much to think about. The old man, who called himself Elijah the Prophet, had said some disturbing things. Was he just a weird nut, a hermit who had gone crazy? Or was he a mystical prophet, eccentric, but a prophet nonetheless? He seemed to know so much about past and future.

The boy also had much to dream about in a world where the mind never slept and took control. As tired as his body was, he tossed restlessly. He was inside something traveling very fast. Then suddenly an explosion. He was flying, sailing peacefully, effortlessly, through the air, almost dream-like, in a trance. Then nothing. He would have the dream many times and always it would end the same. Nothing. A void. An emptiness.

He awakened tired and stiff, his eye swollen shut. But the smell of good food gave him energy to roll out of bed to see Elijah the Prophet frying food over the fire. It looked like pancakes.

"Ah, finally back in the mortal world," said the little man, cackling. "Thought you might sleep yourself into eternity. How's the eye?"

"Sore…smells good. What is it?"

"I call these eternal flapjacks. Made with local ingredients you've never tasted before. "I'll scramble us some wild turkey eggs in a minute. If the taste is too different for your taste buds, you can smother it all in maple syrup, with which you might be more familiar. Then after you've eaten your limit, I'll take you out and introduce you to the mountains."

The breakfast, like the supper last night, did taste good, unique, tantalizing, and absolutely delicious.

Dog led the way, while Jared followed Elijah up a mountain trail, through the forest, made by animals. Both carried a backpack and bedroll. Jared watched the small body in front of him walk with a rolling gait and an occasional hop. Elijah's pointed, narrow brimmed hat, his wild white hair sticking out in all directions, his threadbare, badly fitting clothes, again reminded him of an elf or gnome from a fairy tale.

"Where are we going?" asked Jared.

"Going? Going?" the old man grated, puffing, a bit out of breath, looking back over his shoulder. "For the sake of heaven above. You don't always have to be going somewhere. You must enjoy where you are. Every step you take puts you somewhere different."

They walked on in silence. The Seeker looked around, more alert to his surroundings. Beauty was everywhere. Occasionally, they came to an opening in the forest of fresh smelling pines, where sunshine streamed down upon tall, green grasses and blue and yellow flowers. He saw quaking aspens with their white bark and fluttering leaves in the distance.

They had been climbing up steeply, but now the trail leveled off. Dog quickened his pace and barked three times in a language Elijah understood. "I know, Dog. We're almost to your favorite place."

The forest opened before them, revealing a shining lake, shimmering like liquid silver in the bright sunlight.

"Wow!" exclaimed the boy in wonder.

"Like it, do you?" asked the old man.

"Wow!" said Jared again in answer. "It's absolutely marvelous. So fantastically beautiful. I don't think I've ever seen anything like it, or surely I would remember it. Wouldn't I?"

" I think you would. I thought you might like this place," said the prophet, pleased. "Dog and I like it, too." He turned to look at the boy with his one eye. "I have surmised that you are likely a city boy, but a city boy with the ability to appreciate Mother Nature. And because of that, I have also surmised that you more than likely have some Indian blood in you. That and the fact that your skin is browner than most city kids."

"Tell me about your surmises. Why do you think I'm from the city? Why do you think I'm Native American?" asked the Seeker excitedly.

"Where did you get that expression Native American?" asked the Prophet in return.

"It seems I had a unit on Native American in a school…somewhere, sometime…I don't know."

"Well, Columbus called them Indians, and that's good enough for me. Let's take off our packs and catch a breather. We can talk a bit, then find the best place to camp."

They unloaded their gear and sat in the shade of some quaking aspens, while Dog ran barking happily down to the lake, where he lapped thirstily at its cold, clear water.

"Have a swig," said Elijah, handing Jared a canteen. Then he took several swallows himself. "Now about your questions. I 'm not prophesying or nothing like that, mind. I'm just surmising after observing you."

The old man looked long and hard at the boy with his one good eye. "I figure that you're a city kid by your soft hands and delicate appearance and mannerisms. The way you walk. Your unsureness. I figure you've got some Indian blood in you because your skin is naturally brown, not dark brown, but darker than a totally city kid. Your eyes are brown. Your hair is dark, almost like crow's feathers and you have high cheekbones. In your seeking…who knows? You might find out I am right. An Indian city kid."

The Prophet studied the boy again. "Yep. I've decided, because of your Indianness, to take you on as a project. Teach you about our Earth Mother and Sky Father."

"How do you know so much about Native…about Indians? You're not an Indian, are you?"

"No, I'm not. But I keep telling you that I am a prophet. Besides, I used to live among Indians, now and then."

They were silent awhile, passing the canteen back and forth, until their thirst was quenched. Dog returned from his exploring and flopped down in front of them. The seeker in Jared came forth boldly as he decided to push the questioning. "How long have you been a prophet, Elijah?" he asked.

"A long time," replied the old man. "Long before I came here."

"You mean before you came here to the mountains?"

"No, dummy. Before I came here to this world, called Earth. We're here. So we must have come from somewhere, didn't we?"

Jared looked at him strangely. "I never thought about that before."

The Prophet's eye seemed to pierce into Jared's heart and mind. "Well, let me tell you something important. Since you designated yourself The Seeker, you had better start seeking in earnest. To seek anything properly you must be curious. You must question. You must wonder. Never accept anything by mere surface observation. Look beyond, below, above. Learn to see, hear, taste, smell, and touch. And learn that not all things can be seen. The unseen is more important because it delves into the realms of the eternal, the spiritual.

"Now listen carefully, Seeker. A lot of what I am about to reveal to you can be found by studying that little book you carry in your pocket. Read it each night. Other things you must learn by experience, meditation, and prayer.

"We come from a world of spirits, a pre-existence, before we were born to mortality through our parents. Many of us chose the mission we would fulfill here on earth, others were appointed to their mission. When we die, we return to our real home from whence we came. A curtain or veil is placed on each side of us so we can't remember or look back before our birth and we can't look forward beyond our death. You are in a period of forgetting now. It is called amnesia. For some reason you are going through an additional test. Do you understand what I am saying."

Jared eyed the strange little man in a new light. He studied him. The old man smiled through his beard, reading the boy's thoughts.

"Some of it I understand, and some I don't. But when you talk like that you almost convince me that you might be a prophet."

Elijah cackled his chicken laugh. "Good. You will be a good disciple. I perceive that you are a quick learner. Now back to earthly matters. Have you ever caught a fish?"

"Well...I...er...I don't know."

"Oh, I forgot. You don't remember your past. Well, whether you have or haven't, you are going to catch one today, and you won't need a hundred dollar fishing pole, either. This lake is full of big granddaddies. This place is so high up and secluded that hardly anyone knows it's here. No roads anywhere near and few animal trails. Thick bushes and rough terrain keep the dudes out. Let's set up camp right here. It's as good as any place, isn't it Dog?" Dog barked twice in acknowledgment. "Then, Jared the Seeker, we'll go get us a fishing pole," added the Prophet.

CHAPTER FIVE

They walked to the far end of the lake to a swampy area thick with cattails and willows. Frogs croaked a warning and ducks dipped for moss and bugs, while hawks dove like arrows, wings folded, for minnows.

A pocketknife with many blades for a hundred tasks appeared in Elijah's hand. Jared had not noticed him taking it out, but supposed he got it from his jacket or pants pocket. It was much like his own. The old man selected a seven-foot high willow an inch in diameter at the bottom. He opened the longest blade. "Watch how sharp this is," he instructed.

With three strokes he severed the willow, neat and clean. "One, two, three. Slick as a whistle, huh. Learn a lesson," he explained, looking into the boy's eyes. "Always keep them sharp enough to shave hairs off your arms. It's the dull ones that are dangerous. Course you'll have to wait 'til you are old enough to grow hairs on your arms and other places," he said chuckling.

"How come you don't shave, Elijah?" interrupted Jared.

"Because prophets have beards and long hair, or they aren't true prophets. Besides, it wastes time shaving and getting haircuts and all that. I like to get up and about. Now pay attention to the lesson I'm giving you. We are talking about tools and willows and fishing, not about hair. Now watch."

He rounded off the handle end of the willow. Then he trimmed off the other end at about seven feet. He notched a groove around it. A wad of catgut appeared in his hand. He tied it firmly around the notched part, lay the pole on the ground, strung out about forty feet of line, then cut it off. He pulled a fish hook from his hat and tied it on the line. "Now, Jared my boy, we are ready to bait the hook. These willows will bend nearly in half. It's almost impossible to break them. Don't need no fancy store bought pole. We'll find something big and juicy to put on the hook, so we won't need a sinker. See that flat rock over there," he said, pointing. "Turn it over."

Jared did as instructed. "Yuck," he exclaimed. "All sorts of creepy crawlers here."

"That's the fish food; bugs, insects, and worms. They love them. Lots of protein. If ever you are lost and starving, you can eat this stuff. Here is a marvelous, huge, juicy worm. The big ones will snap him up, even fight over him."

Jared cringed as the prophet put the worm on the hook. "A little squeamish, are you?" cackled the old man. "That's the city kid in you. The Indian part of you will adjust. I'll show you how to do all of this once, then you're on your own."

He handed the pole to the boy. "Now, Seeker, you're ready to catch yourself a fish. There are some whoppers in this lake. Go stand on the big dead tree sticking out in the water. Whip the line out as far as it will go. I'll cut myself a pole. Can't let you have all the fun."

Jared walked carefully out on the log and awkwardly threw the line out into the water. In less time than he could catch his breath, a jerk on his line almost pulled the pole out of his hands. It startled him so much he nearly fell off the log. "I got one, Elijah. I got one!" he shouted excitedly.

The old man ran to the excited boy. "Alright now keep the end of your pole pointed up at the sky. Keep the line tight. That's it. You don't have one of those fancy reel gadgets and we don't have a net. So walk back carefully off the log. That's it. Keep your pole high. Now move down to the shallow water. Now walk back, keeping your line tight. Pull him up on land. You got him! Good job!"

Elijah bent down and grabbed the flopping fish by the gills, then removed the hook. "What a beauty! A granddaddy. Must be a six or eight pounder. It's a rainbow trout. See the colors on its sides," he said, showing the boy. "It will provide delicious eating.

Now the work comes. The cleaning. Watch while I show you this once, then you are on your own."

The pocket knife, large blade opened, appeared in his hand, while he held the fish firmly with the other. "You start at its rear end and slit the belly like this, then pull out the guts."

"Yuck," said Jared, pulling a face.

"You'll get over it, son, as soon as you've cleaned your first one. Now just slush him around in the water and clean a little more. When we get back to camp, I'll show you how to fillet him, so we don't have to worry about picking out a lot of bones. Better to cook smaller fish whole, but the big ones like this you can fillet. Okay, lesson over. Was it fun catching your fish?"

"Was it fun? I can't wait to catch another. Wow! That is what I call real fun."

"Okay, get back to your fishing, while I get my pole and line ready. I can't wait to get started, either," said Elijah, smiling through his beard.

Jared ended the day with five fish, Elijah four. As they carried them to camp strung on a willow, the old man sang a song in his high pitched voice.

> "I love to fish in the bright sunshine
> And watch the fish pull on my line
> Then to take him off my hook
> And back to camp my fish to cook."

The boy laughed joyfully and began to sing along with the old man.

CHAPTER SIX

The fish tasted delicious. Elijah had filleted the big one expertly, while Jared watched. Then he cooked it over the hot coals of the campfire. He was smoking the rest in small strips. He had also baked a batch of sourdough bread in a small iron, lidded skillet, from makings he had brought in his pack. He pointed to the fish he was smoking. "It will be jerky," he explained. "It will last almost forever. Jerky was originally made from buffalo meat, then venison. But now it is any kind of dried or smoked meat. I prefer it dried gradually in the hot sun."

"How did you learn to do so much; to know how to do so many things?" asked Jared.

"Trial and error, my boy. That's what is called experience. The best teacher there is. When you live alone and have to survive, you pick up a lot of skills."

"By the way, Elijah, I've been so interested in this pretty place, these mountains and all, that I forgot to ask you where this is. Where are we?" asked the Seeker, handing Dog some fish scraps, which he chewed noisily and gratefully.

"Rocky Mountains is where we are. This particular portion is in the state called Colorado."

"I don't think I've ever been in Colorado. I mean, when I was whoever I was before."

"Don't worry about that right now. Since our bellies are full, I thought I'd make us some music. First, I have to make a musical instrument. Observe!"

He pulled a foot long piece of green willow from his oversized pocket. "I cut this special back at the swamp. Now I spit on it continuously while I tap it with my knife, like this. Again and again, I spit and tap. Now the green bark is loosening. I twist it gently, ever so gently, so as not to split it. And I slip the bark off the willow.

"Next, I cut the end to taper, to blow on with my lips. Then I cut a couple of angular notches. Okay, now I slip the bark carefully back onto the willow and notch little slits over the other notches. And here we have a flute."

"Incredible," said Jared, fascinated. "Absolutely incredible."

"Thank you." Said the old man, chuckling. "You will now hear music of the angels. Sit back. Relax. Watch the dance of the dragonflies out over the lake. Watch them dance to my music. They will bob up and down, skim the water in circles and perform pirouettes. See how their wings look like cellophane reflecting the sun. Gossamer wings." He began a catchy tune.

> Wings of sorrow
> Wings of light
> Soaring high
> Then out of sight

He cackled his unique laugh. "In case you haven't noticed I am a poet, a song composer, and musician, as well as a prophet.

Jared laughed joyfully with him.

Then Elijah became serious. He wet his lips, lifted the willow flute to his mouth and began playing a mystical, melancholy tune. It entranced the boy. A magic spell overcame him. The sun sank in a rose colored sky to the west, while the moon rose above the trees to the east, and formed a golden path on the lake, a path that Jared felt he could walk on and keep going right up to the moon.

By the time the old man lay down his flute, the boy's eyes had closed in sleep, the music still playing in his head. Gently, Elijah lifted him onto his blanket and tucked another over him.

CHAPTER SEVEN

Terror entered Jared's senses while he slept. A smell! A musty, evil stench. A gutteral grunting. His eyes popped open. Two large yellow eyes, the red coals of the campfire reflected in them, stared at him inches from his face. Pure fear flooded his brain. His hair spiked as though filled with static electricity. He tried to cry out, but his voice froze in his throat. The horrible apparition began to drag him from his blankets by one arm, then hugged him in its huge, vise-like, hairy arms with the strength of a gigantic gorilla. It gashed his shoulder and arm from elbow to wrist with its angry, long claws. The pain seared through him like hot needles. The stinking breath of the monster was in his nostrils. He could almost taste it.

Somehow he found his voice. "Help, Elijah! Elijah, help me!" he screamed. Dog awakened and with a mighty leap, attacked the beast, snarling deep in his throat. The huge creature swatted Dog away like a fly with its large paws. Dog fell limply in a silent heap. The beast stood up on its hind legs, shaking Jared like a rag doll. In the moonlight, Jared now realized his adversary was a huge bear of at least nine feet tall. "Elijah help!" he cried desperately.

The little man was up in a flash. He grabbed a hot stick from the fire and poked the burning end into the silver-tipped grizzly's bald face. It shook Jared again, nearly crushing his ribs, then dropped him to the ground and stepped forward to attack Elijah. The prophet raised both his gnarly hands high in the air, like a cheerleader and chanted strange, unknown words. The great grizzly began to sway back and forth, towering dangerously over the little man.

"Haere, haere, haere, ki te po," Elijah repeated three times.

Amazingly, Jared understood the old man's chant. He was saying, "Go, go, go, into the night." The huge beast shook its head
several times, then suddenly dropped to all four feet, turned, and
ambled off toward the lake and into the shadows.

Elijah turned to the injured boy. "That bear won't be back.
Are you all right, my boy," he asked, kneeling beside Jared.

"I think…I think he hurt my shoulder, Elijah," Jared replied
weakly, body trembling uncontrollably.

"Ohhh, he hurt you indeed. First to stop the bleeding." He
tore some cloth from his bedroll. "I must put a tourniquet around
your upper arm. There. Now I'll clean it up a bit with some me-
dicinal alcohol from my kit. It'll hurt."

"Oh. Oh. It does sting some," wailed Jared. "How do you
know the bear won't come back?" He glanced around, looking for
his attacker.

"I know. That was an ancient chant used at funerals long ago.
Even animals understand it. They know it carries a curse of death,
if they don't obey."

A pitiful whining came from Dog. "Did the bear hurt you,
too?" asked the boy.

"Oh, poor Dog," said Elijah, running to him. "I forgot about
you in the excitement. Poor Dog, you were so brave. Thank you.
The bear got your shoulder, too. Let me look at it."

During the next hours, the little man was back and forth between Jared and Dog, cleaning wounds, wrapping, doctoring. He
knelt on the ground and said a short prayer, asking for strength.
Jared the Seeker began to mumble incoherently. Elijah felt the
boy's forehead. Fever. I must get the boy and Dog back to the
cabin where I have herbs and other medicines, he thought with
anguish and determination.

CHAPTER EIGHT

Jared the Seeker awoke to sunlight through the cabin door. He blinked and looked around at his surroundings to get his bearings. "I seem to be back in Elijah the Prophet's cabin, but surely I must have died and gone to heaven because I smell the most heavenly roast turkey. How can that be?"

The old man's cackle reassured him. "Ah, he lives. He has finally returned from the world of dreams and spirits."

"How can I smell roast turkey?" Jared asked, somewhat bewildered.

"It is true. You are back in the home of Elijah the Prophet. You smell turkey because it is roasting over my fireplace. I have basted it with real butter, kept cold in my creek, and also with scrumptious wild berries. It will be ready shortly."

"Where in the world did you get a turkey?"

Elijah laughed joyfully, enjoying himself. "Right in my backyard. Wild turkeys and pine hens are plentiful here. We are so high up they have hardly seen humans. I build nooses and trap them. They almost walk right into my arms. I don't use a gun up here. It might attract unwanted company. I only use it down below for pheasants, quail, deer, rabbits, and a variety of wild food. I'll take you down when you're healed and teach you to shoot."

Jared felt a warm licking on his cheek. He turned to see the huge Golden Retriever smiling at him and wagging his fan-like tail. "Oh, Dog, it's so good to see that you're okay," he said, reaching out his good arm to stroke Dog under his chin. Dog licked his face again affectionately.

"Dog heals faster than boy," stated Elijah. "He has been up

and about, just limps slightly, but he will get stronger. How do you feel, my boy?"

Jared started to get up. "Ohhhh," he moaned, and fell back on the old bed. "My ribs ache and I'm stiff all over."

"Does that mean that Dog and I will eat turkey by ourselves?"

"Not on your life. Give me a few minutes and I'll have plenty of eating strength," said the Seeker, swinging his legs off the bed. "I'll go outside and get rid of some water, then I'll wash up and be ready. I'm hungry as a bear," he added laughing and ruefully remembering another starved bear that nearly killed and ate him.

"Take your time," said Elijah, helping him to stand. "You'll probably be lightheaded for a few minutes, you lost some blood. Also, I need to apologize to you and Dog."

"Why?"

"It was my fault, the bear. I should have known better and hung the fish in a tree down by the lake. It was the fish smell that attracted him to our camp."

"By the way, how did a little guy like you get me and Dog back here to the cabin?"

"I may be little, but my strength is the strength of many because I live a pure life," he replied with a mischievous twinkle in his eye. "And because my mountain skills as a craftsman allowed me to build a travois."

"What's that?"

"A travois is like a stretcher dragged along the ground. The Indians made them to help haul their belongings when they moved camp to a new spot. It's made of two long poles tied together with shorter ones across and a makeshift harness to pull it. Like a wagon without wheels. And so, I got you and Dog back here with a minimum of effort on my part and a lot of help from the Great One above. You've got an infection in your wounds, which I am treating with herbs and poultices.

"Now go and take care of your toilet duties and get yourself back here to our table and a feed fit for a Seeker, a Prophet, and a loyal dog.

The healing process was slow and painful. Each night, Jared cried himself to sleep with pain from the three deep gashes that ran from his shoulder to his elbow. He sobbed silently, hoping the old man would not hear him. He could find only a few half-comfortable positions; on his back and partially on his good side. Each morning, he awakened stiff, sore, and tired, and every night, before bed, the old man changed the bandages and treated his wounds with the herbs and poultice. Gradually, the Prophet nursed him back to where he had strength enough to stay up most of the day and walk down to the creek and wash himself with his good hand.

"You should have had those wounds sewed up," Elijah concluded. "But there was nowhere I could take you myself. They are healing fine, but will leave scars. Three stripes from shoulder to elbow to remember old bear by. He sure clawed you up some, alright."

He about squeezed me to pieces, too. I still hurt all over. But not as much. I won't mind scars. They will remind me, also, of how lucky I am to still be here," stated Jared, sounding braver than he felt.

"That's the spirit, my boy. You've got spunk for a city kid."

"You still think I'm a city kid, Elijah?"

"I know you are. You'll see I'm right when you find your other self again. But before I send you off, I'll make a mountain boy out of you."

Speaking of my other self," interrupted Jared hesitantly, "shouldn't I get on with my seeking when I am healed?"

"Nope. Not yet. I've still got a lot to teach you and you've got a lot to learn. I'll tell you when it is time to go." The old man looked at him intensely with his one eye. "The first and most important thing you need to learn, something most folks never learn, is that the important seeking is always an inward search in the mind and heart. Thinking, tossing around ideas, forming opinions, establishing convictions. The outward seeking is just a byproduct. Now you do some thinking about what I just told you, while you are healing. No hurry. Use the time for thinking."

CHAPTER NINE

The scars faded from scarlet to pink to white. Weeks had passed, until one day Elijah said, "Are you ready to start therapy?"

"What therapy?" asked Jared, somewhat bewildered.

"Raise your arm above your shoulder."

"Why?"

"Raise it!" commanded the old man.

"Ohhhh. It hurts," groaned Jared, wincing with pain.

"That's what I mean. Therapy. The bear tore the ligaments and muscle in your shoulder. If we don't get started now you could lose some movement in that shoulder and arm." The Prophet took a firm grip on Jared's arm with both his powerful hands and slowly began to rotate the arm around, back and forth, and up and down. The boy screamed in pain. "Stop! Oh stop. It's killing me."

"We will start slowly, twice a day," explained Elijah, kindly. "It will hurt a great deal at first. But it has to be done. I don't want a cripple on my hands. Better a little pain now than a useless arm."

So began the therapy. Every morning and again at night, the old man worked on the boys limb while Jared screamed and yelled. Then he rubbed the arm and shoulder with a strong smelling liquid.

"What's that stuff?" Jared inquired, wrinkling his nose.

"Horse liniment and it will sting like crazy for awhile, but it will sooth the shoulder and maybe you can get some sleep."

"Yowee! Sting is right!" Gradually, the soothing took effect. "You're right, Elijah. It does help."

"Course I'm right," the shaggy, one eyed, old man exclaimed confidently.

Jared studied the strange little man, with his wild hair, beard, and funny hat that he even slept in. He decided to ask the question he had often thought about. "Elijah, what happened to your eye?"

"None of your business," shot back the Prophet.

"Well, make it my business. I would like to know," Jared insisted.

"It happened a long time ago. I would rather leave it in the past. No need of rehashing things we can't change."

The boy studied him again for a long time in strained silence, then decided to drop the subject.

The yelling and screaming lessened during the therapy sessions and gradually subsided altogether. "Ready to chop wood now?" asked the Prophet several weeks later.

"I can give it a try."

"Good, I'll show you how and make a mountain boy out of you yet."

They walked around to the back of the cabin to an already sizeable pile of split wood neatly stacked against the cabin. There was a stump with an axe stuck in it.

"This here is a chopping block," instructed Elijah as he grasped the axe by the handle and jerked it free from the stumps grasp. "Feel the blade. Run your thumb lightly over it. Sharp, huh? Always keep it that way. Stand back now and watch."

He stood a log, about six inches in diameter and a foot and a half long, on end on the stump. Then he gripped the axe handle tightly in both hands and swung it in a smooth arc over his head. Whump! It hit the log dead center and the two halves parted neatly, falling on each side of the stump. "Okay," he said, handing the axe to Jared. "Your turn."

The boy swung and hit the next log in the center, but the axe head just embedded itself in the log. He winced as pain seared his shoulder.

"Still bother you a little?" asked the Prophet.

"A little."

"Just practice awhile on your own without me peering over your shoulder. I'll take care of some other chores," Elijah said as he waddled away.

Gradually, the pain and stiffness began to leave the boy's shoulder. He enjoyed the feel of the axe as it hit squarely into the top of each log, and felt exhilaration as he began to split them in one swing.

Suddenly, a day later, while he was splitting wood, the sky darkened. A few drops of rain hit his face, then began to spatter with regularity.

"Come on, let's go inside," yelled Elijah from around the corner of the cabin. "These mountain rains come fast and furious"

"I'm getting the hang of this," Jared stated jubilantly as they entered the cabin. "I think I've got the feel of that downward swing. You know..to give it that extra power so the log splits neatly in one swing."

"Good. I had a feeling you might just be a swift learner for a city kid," teased the old man, chicken cackling at Jared's chagrin at the deliberate insult.

The rain gushed from the sky steadily in heavy drops, rapping at the thatched roof, while the fresh smell of wet pines and other forest odors filled the cabin. Soon, the sky became so dark Elijah had to light the kerosene lantern on the rickety, three-legged table. The air cooled refreshingly.

"Don't you wish you had some conveniences, like electricity and plumbing and some comforts, you know?" the boy ventured as they sat and relaxed, listening to the rain.

"Nope. This cabin is like Dog here. Like an old loyal companion," he stated, reaching down and scratching the huge Retriever's head. Dog licked his hand in thanks. "Now that you know I'm a poet, I'll recite my poem in honor of this house. So listen up.

"Log Cabin
Hardened clay between logs
Logs gray from years before

Dirt roof mingled with weeds
Worn floor
One window
One door
Time holds it together
And it stands forever more."

Jared looked at the old man silently for a long time, saying nothing.

"What's the matter," queried Elijah. "Don't like my poem?"

"Sure I do. It's just that…well, it's just that I can't figure you out, Elijah. You live like a mountain hermit; you know all about Indians, and seem to follow their beliefs. Yet you study the Bible and believe in its teachings. What are you?"

"I am a prophet. I've told you a hundred times." Elijah replied, exasperated.

They were quiet again, listening to the rain, mentally wondering about each other, until the boy spoke. "I know you are my friend," Jared began quietly. "You saved my life twice. I don't know what I would have done, if I hadn't found your cabin." He looked hard into Elijah's eye. "But I still can't believe you are a prophet, I don't believe there are prophets now days. This is the twentieth century, isn't it?"'

The old man looked hurt. He fidgeted on his chair-box, scratched his forearm, and pulled his beard. Silently, he reached down and ruffled Dog's fur. "I am sorry you don't believe because I am a prophet. He who does not believe is lost. And you are still lost, Jared the Seeker," he added hesitantly. "I didn't always live up here alone. I have had an acquaintance with education. I know books. I know people. I can look inside them."

This was the most the strange little man would reveal of himself, but he went on talking nervously, more than usual. "If you think I am not a prophet, explain to me how my messenger, Great Horned Owl led you here and talked in your mind. How did I know you were The Seeker and had been expecting you? If a prophet doubts himself, then he is no longer a prophet. The big difference between you and me is not our age; it is that you are a doubter and I am a believer. I didn't ask to be a prophet. The mantle just fell upon me," he explained, unconsciously adjusting the black patch over his bad eye.

Jared felt bad that he had hurt his friend's feelings. He tried to soften matters. "There are a lot of things I can't explain. Maybe Owl is your trained pet. Maybe..." his voice trailed off. "There is something strange, that I know for sure. When you entranced the bear, that night, using strange language, I understood what you said."

Elijah looked deep inside the boy with his good eye. Jared felt the Prophet was inside his soul, knowing completely about him, knowing him from a former time, another previous life. Could it be? He had never felt so strange before, like he was transformed back, back, back before there was such a thing as time.

"Simple," replied the Prophet. "Speaking in tongues and interpretations of tongues. Me, the spokesman. You, the interpreter. It happened quite commonly in ancient times. Why not now?"

"Another thing," Jared began, wanting to believe, wanting to talk, to listen, to learn from whoever or whatever this man, who called himself a prophet, really was. "While I was unconscious, I dreamed. I was in a big, beautiful house in a large city. There was a well-dressed man and woman, and two girls a little older than me. It seemed that these were my parents and sisters. My family. They treated me politely at first, but like a stranger. I belonged and yet I did not belong. I was somehow out of place. Then suddenly these people. My family, started looking at me like I was an alien. They treated me like an outcast. I no longer believed. Then the dream ended.

The rain came heavier, in torrents. The lamp burned lower, grew dim. An overwhelming melancholy wave, almost visible in impact, swept over Jared the Seeker.

"I could interpret much of your dream, but you are not a believer...yet. And your dream is of the future. The future is to learn from, as is the past. So I must not tamper with it. But think upon your dreams. They come to us for a reason. In that Bible you carry, it tells us Joel, Chapter Two, Verses twenty eight to thirty two, 'Your old men shall dream dreams, your young men shall see visions...and I will show wonders in the heavens and earth.'

"You can read that for yourself later. In fact, we are going to start reading every night. We cannot forget the mind part of your education. Everything, every act, every creation, every accomplishment is first conceived in the mind, conscious, subconscious, or unconscious.

"Our fuel ration for the lamp is burning down. Let's conserve and turn into our beds to enjoy the cadence of the rain. And to think and perchance to dream." He looked at the Seeker, and added, "And try hard to become believers."

CHAPTER TEN

It rained. And it rained. And it rained. Five days and still raining steadily. Small rivulets trickled on all sides of the cabin and down the mountain. The roof of the cabin leaked, but they patched it with mud and weeds.

Ancient smells seeped out of the ground from eons of leaves, pine needles, bark, and bones of creatures long since turned to powder and becoming a part of the eternally rejuvenating earth. Jared the Seeker conjured visions of Jarassaic, Triassic, and other eras of creatures, their massive bodies crashing trees, crushing bushes in their quest for food. Enormous birds, the size of Beech craft airplanes, came swooping out of the sky. Butterflies with iridescent blue wings as large as kites lit on giant peach colored flowers. There were no humans to interfere. No human sounds. No bells, buzzers, sirens, motors, machines, just the sounds of creatures, water, and wind.

A human voice interceded into his thoughts. "Sorry," he said. "My mind was somewhere else. What did you say?"

"I said it's your turn to fix the meals next week, starting tomorrow," Elijah repeated, bluntly.

"But I don't know how," Jared retorted, batting his eyelids over chocolate colored eyes.

"You'd better learn fast or we'll starve. I'm tired of fixing. I am now on strike. From here on, we rotate every other week."

And so the boy learned to cook. There was nothing in cans, bottles, or packages. He had learned that Elijah went into the small village of Paradise about once every two or three months, and traded some of his craft items for flour, sugar, salt, and seeds for a small garden in front of the cabin, which Jared had helped plant and consisted of carrots, radishes, beans, peas, lettuce, cantaloupes, watermelon, and cucumbers. They dried and smoked meats, berries, fruit, and nuts. They hunted, trapped, and fished. His first meals were mostly salads and cold put-togethers. Elijah never complained, but about the sixth meal, he suggested, "We need a something hot. You'd better make us a stew and some kind of bread.

The first stew was like mush; the first bread soggy dough, and the second loaf hard as a boot heel. But he was learning and had discovered that one of the best ways of learning was by doing. Elijah was patient through it all. "Come here, I want to measure you," coaxed the Prophet, while the rain still fell.

"What for?" questioned Jared, wiping bread dough from his hands.

"For new clothes. That shirt is thin as toilet paper and your pants are as threadbare as cobwebs. I've got some nice buckskin I've tanned from deer hides. I'll make you an outfit like Daniel Boone, Kit Carson, and those fellers used to wear. You can watch me and learn how to cut, sew, and create clothing."

The finished product was marvelous and fit perfectly.

"Now you're beginning to look like a mountain boy," said the old Prophet, appraising his work. "You have acquired some muscle in those arms and legs. The bear claw scars have healed nicely. You are losing your city smell." The old man held his nose, just to irritate his young friend. Jared gave him a sidelong glance and smiled. "When the rain quits," Elijah went on, "I'll teach you to shoot. I have two guns; a twelve-gauge shotgun and a beautiful Winchester thirty-thirty carbine. I can shoot the eye out of a squirrel with it.

"Like I told you, I don't like to shoot, unless necessary. It attracts attention. But our meat supply is getting low. We'll go down to lower country and get us some rabbits, quail, and pheasants. Maybe nail us a deer, if we're lucky."

"You amaze me, Elijah," said the boy. "The things you know how to do."

"When you've lived alone as long as I have, you just rely on

yourself." Then he quickly added, "And, of course, the Man upstairs, the Creator of it all. He has been around to help in some
real pinches."

"Thank you for these pants and jacket. I couldn't buy anything near as nice as this in a store." Jared added gratefully. "And
thank you again for taking me in and teaching me so much."

"You are welcome, Jared the Seeker. I hope I am preparing you
well for your seeking, not just to find your identity, but forever. To
me, you see, seeking is learning and it should never end. It is a
matter of eternal progression. We should develop a deep, rich hunger
and thirst for learning that can never be satisfied or quenched."

They spent many hours reading, each from his own Bible.
Jared asked questions, which they discussed, rather than Elijah
merely answering them. Then they took turns reading aloud from
the Bible and Shakespeare. Elijah quoted passages from great phi-
losophers, such as Socrates, Plato, Decartes; government and economic thinkers, like Thomas Paine, Adam Smith, Patrick Henry,
Abraham Lincoln. Religious men, like St. Thomas Achenes, St.
Francis of Assisi, and Thomas a Kempis. During these discussions,
Dog lay comfortably at their feet, seeming to enjoy human conversation, as though understanding much of what was said.

Elijah knew much about great playwrights, musicians, and artists. His knowledge of history, geography, peoples, and cultures
seemed endless. Jared marveled. He wondered from where this strange
little man's book learning had come. But Elijah would not talk of
the past. Jared found himself observing Him, trying to figure him
out. Sometimes the old man was flippant, rather silly acting. Weird.
Then other times he was a man of vast wisdom. A prophet.

On the ninth night, the rain ceased. The stars came out. The
moon lit up the world like a magic lantern, then the sun woke
them up, blinking in its brightness. Steam rose in waves, making
the mountains and trees below appear as a mirage. The earth was
fresh, cleansed, and so were their spirits. New hope. New dreams.
A new rejuvenated world to be explored for the first time.

CHAPTER ELEVEN

They traveled to the lake to bathe after their long confinement in the cabin. When they reached the clearing where the bear had attacked them, Elijah asked, "Are you frightened, being here again in this spot?"

"Maybe just a bit worried," answered Jared, looking warily around.

Suddenly, Dog growled deep in his throat, neck and back hackles at attention.

"He's over there. Dog spotted him," Elijah whispered, pointing.

"Who is over there" And where?" Jared replied fearfully.

"The bear. Look straight across the lake. There, on the beach in front of that tallest pine. See him watching us?"

The boy looked, scanning. Finally, he spotted his old adversary. "I see him now," he quaked. "It wouldn't take him long to get around here, would it?"

"Not to worry, my boy," assured the old man confidently. "He will never bother us again. Notice his posture? He is sitting on his haunches observing us, as if to say, "I know you. Respect me and my realms and I will respect yours." Then as if to prove his confidence, the Prophet handed Jared a home made bar of soap. "Get your clothes off and let's get in that invigorating water and get our bodies clean and refreshed.

They stripped off their clothes and dashed out into the shallow water, Dog following, barking joyfully. They were in water up to their waists when Jared felt goose bumps rising on his body and he began to shake.

"Dip down in the water to your neck," Elijah advised. "Once you're in, it won't be so cold."

Jared discovered he was right. They soaped themselves, passing it back and forth, gratefully lathering away the musty smell of idleness in the cabin.

"It makes nice suds, even in this cold water…the soap, I mean," remarked Jared. "How did you make it?"

"Oh, lots of animal fat melted down, rendered out, and mixed with a little of this and a pinch of that, then heated and poured into my own clay molds. Not bad, huh? I'll show you how sometime. Now to rinse off, we have ourselves a brisk swim," and he swam away, stroking quickly, showing the way.

Back on shore, they let the sun dry their bodies, savoring the warm rays. Dog shook his long, golden fur, particles of water gleaming like diamonds on his body, then laid down on a warm, grassy spot and proceeded to sleep and dream, contented, while Elijah produced a long comb and began to pull the snarls from his beard. Then he parted his long hair in the middle and combed it out straight on each side.

Jared watched, amused at the little man's unabashed movements and the fact his dear old companion had finally removed his pointed "fedora." He wondered again about this eccentric, old gentleman, and the things he had heard from him and seen him do. Finally, he gazed across the lake and saw the silver-tipped grizzly still watching them. This was all very strange. He turned to admire the beauty of his surroundings, which made him feel a part of a dream or fairy tale.

The old man observed him in return. "You like this place, don't you?" he inquired.

"Yes, very much. I feel I should stay forever. In this moment, this time," declared Jared, seriously.

"This is my Utopia, my Shangri La. I never want to leave. This is my mortal refuge. My bath tub, my gymnasium, my cold storage locker, my food mart. You name it. I am glad you like it, too."

They rested on the grass near Dog, who wagged his tail in friendly fashion, eyes half closed. Quiet, soft, pleasant sounds came from around them. A lone cricket chirped from deep in the shadows. A fish jumped, cleared the water, then splashed back in. Jared rolled over and watched the expanding circles in the otherwise still lake. A Mountain Bluebird called from the far end of the lake near the willows, while a faint, hardly detectable breeze rustled the leaves of the quaking aspens behind them. Serenity. That was the word Elijah had taught him. Now he understood it.

"What are you thinking?" asked the Prophet, breaking the silence.

"Tell me, Elijah, have you ever thought of what went into making a stone an ordinary rock?"

The old man rolled on his side, his one eye piercing the boy's. "I have wondered and pondered upon many things, but not that particular one. A very good thought, my boy. Very good, indeed. Scientists, geologists could explain the chemical composition of a rock, and probably hand out some explanation of the process, but I think only the Creator could tell of what went into its making over millions of years, by way of our time.

"Albert Einstein, one of the great geniuses, put it best. He said the most beautiful thing we can experience is the mysterious." He looked again into Jared's eyes. "I believe you are becoming a true seeker. You are learning. You are asking questions that go beyond the obvious. You are learning to use your spiritual eyes and ears. Keep it up, Jared the Seeker. The deepest search is within our own minds.

"Let's get dressed and head back to the cabin. I am hungry. How about you, Dog?" Dog awakened fully and barked with agreement.

"My turn to hustle us some grub," stated the old man, plopping his funny pointed hat on his damp hair.

CHAPTER TWELVE

"Today, we will go hunting," announced the Prophet as he rolled off his makeshift bed on the floor, stretched and yawned. Then he added, "I mean hunting with guns. As I said, I don't like using them for many reasons. One is that it gives us unfair advantage over the creatures. But there is need for meat to be stored for the winter. We need to take our backpacks and an extra sack, in case we are lucky and get a lot of game. Down on the lower hills are plenty of grouse, quail, pheasants, rabbits, squirrels, you name it. Lots of fat, juicy meat waiting. I'll show you how to shoot and seldom miss."

Elijah demonstrated how to load the shotgun, carry it safely, and hold it tight against his shoulder to reduce kick. The first pheasant flew right up from under Jared's feet. The sudden flutter of wings startled him so he rushed off the shot and missed.

"If he's flying directly away from you, like that one, you've got plenty of time to get off your shot," instructed Elijah, patiently. "He is rising, gaining altitude, so shoot slightly above him. If he is flying across in front of you, lead him a little."

Jared learned quickly. They took turns and bagged many flying and running creatures. Their game bag was heavy and they were weary, when Elijah announced, "We'd better head back to the cabin."

"But we're doing great," protested Jared. "We can shoot a lot more game; the day isn't half over."

"I know how much you're enjoying the hunt, my boy, but a hunt is not for enjoyment alone. It is for our need, and we have plenty. Beyond that, it becomes mere sport hunting, which I don't believe in. Besides, if our game bag becomes much heavier two skinny guys like us won't be able to carry it back." He glanced at Jared. "I should say one skinny guy – me. You have put on some bulk and muscle. You are filling out to a husky young feller. This mountain living agrees with you."

Jared filled with warmth at the compliment. Now he enjoyed the feel of the axe in his hands as it bit into a log, a shovel as it stabbed the soil, a full pack as it brought out the sweat that trickled down his back and from his arm pits.

They had entered the clearing below the cabin, when Elijah whispered, "Stop! There, see it? A young buck deer, right ahead. Here, take the rifle and get him!"

"I've never shot something like that. It's eyes…it is looking right at us. I don't want to shoot it."

"It is offering itself to us, boy. That's why it is standing there, looking at us. Here, you need to experience the rifle. It doesn't kick like the shotgun. Shoot for his heart, right behind his front legs. Put the spot you're aiming at right on top of the bead sight."

Jared hesitantly took the Winchester and did as instructed.

"Now, squeeze the trigger gently, slowly let out your breath, then hold it."

The shot went off without Jared hardly realizing it. The deer dropped in its tracks. They ran to it. The old man pulled out his knife and slit its throat to bleed, so the meat would be fresh and juicy.

"Good shot, Jared. No suffering. He was dead immediately." He glanced at the boy and saw tears glistening in his eyes. "It is good that you can cry at the death of one of god's creatures. Killing is not a pleasant task and never should be taken lightly, not even at the death of the smallest and least significant creature. But this deer offered itself to us for our nourishment. Kneel here by me while I sing the song of the deer. I learned it from my Indian friends."

The old man half chanted, half sang, in a high pitched mournful lament. When he finished, he turned to Jared and put his hand lightly on his shoulder. "Did you understand?"

"Yes," agreed Jared the Seeker. "I understood, more than just words. It was beautiful, Elijah. I now know many more things, also."

They worked hard, cleaning the entrails from their game, plucking feathers, pulling, and skinning. "Now we must dig a pit and bury all their insides and return them to rejuvenate Mother Earth." Next, they quartered and cut the flesh of the animals into strips, then smoked it over a fire on sticks. Other portions were salted heavily and stretched out on rocks in the sun to dry. They were tired when work was done, at peace with themselves and all the earth.

"Let's go down to the creek and wash up," suggested Elijah, grabbing soap and a towel.

"Thanks for teaching me so much," said Jared, quietly, eyes down, his dark hair now grown to his shoulders, bangs nearly over his eyes. He looked and thought more like a muscular, bronze Indian everyday. The Prophet smiled warmly.

Jared knelt to wash in the creek and suddenly felt a hot sting before he heard the buzzing. A timber rattler had struck and sank its fangs deep into his wrist! "Snake, Elijah," he howled, frightened, rising and holding his wrist. "A rattle snake bit me!" The guilty, three-foot long snake raced to hide under a rock.

The old Prophet moved like a lightning strike. He snatched up the reptile by the tail, the buttons rattling for a fight, swung it around over his head like a lariat, and snapped it like a bullwhip. The snake fell limply to the ground, mouth gaping open dangerously, needle-like fangs exposed. Viciously, Elijah stomped on its head twice to make sure it was dead, then raced to Jared, whose face was ash-gray with horror.

"Let me look!" Elijah grabbed the wrist, sucked hard at the two holes, and spit several times. "Let's get you into the cabin, lying down, so the poison won't spread through your body too much. You're going to be very sick and suffer terrible pain, but you'll be okay later. There are few deaths from rattlers, unless you are bitten on the face or neck."

Jared's wrist was swollen and angry by the time they reached the cabin. The Prophet put him in bed and covered him with a blanket, though the weather was hot. The arm continued to swell. Soon, the boy suffered chills and fever. He became delirious, mumbling incoherently, while Elijah prepared and applied herbs and poultices. Though tired, he sat with Jared all through the afternoon, evening, and night, chanting strange songs.

CHAPTER THIRTEEN

Jared opened his eyes. It was dark. A fire flickered in the fireplace, causing eerie shadows to dance around the walls and across the foot worn floor. Again, he was lost. It took him several minutes to orient himself. He moaned as pain shot through his arm. He looked at the swollen, blue limb. It was alien. It did not belong to him. Then he remembered the snake. He moaned again, his throat dry. "Elijah," he called weakly.

"Right here, my boy," The old man rose from the floor and peeked over at the wounded boy. He had placed his bedroll next to Jared's bed. "Good to see you come around."

"How long have I been out?"

"A night and a day. It is just turning into the second night."

Tears came. Jared let them flow freely, letting out his pain and frustration. "Why are all these bad things happening to me?" he sobbed. "Why? Why me? I wake up in a pine tree, not knowing who I am or how I got there. A bear tried to eat me alive, then a rattlesnake gets me. Why so many things to me, Elijah? It's like I am in a bad dream and I keep hoping to wake up."

The old man rose, sat on the side of the bed and looked at his charge tenderly. "Feeling a little sorry for yourself?" he asked, lowly.

"You're darned right I am. I'm just a kid and I'll bet I've had more bad things happen to me than ten kids, Look at the size of my arm!"

"You should have seen it at its swollen peak. Looked like a balloon about to burst. I am proud to tell you, kid or no kid, you are more of a man than most men I've known. You're right. You have had more problems than most. Shakespeare said in Hamlet that problems like yours, 'come not single spies, but in battal-ions.'

"You ask why these things happen. None can answer that. But I think all things happen for a reason. In the scriptures, we have been reading, it hints that before great blessings are to be bestowed, there are great trials to be endured. A Chinese proverb says, 'The gem cannot be polished without friction, nor man perfected without trials.'"

The compliment and the words eased the boy's crying, though his arm throbbed like hammer blows. "Then I'm getting better?"

"A day or two and you won't believe this ever happened." Then the Prophet added quietly, as though half speaking himself, "Once, I felt sorry for myself."

"You did?" asked Jared, showing new interest.

"Yep, a long time ago. It was the sorry that drove me up here to the mountains, away from people. I suppose it made me kind of different, like I am now."

"Will you tell me all about it?" asked Jared, eagerly.

"Nope. But I'll tell you that it all worked out for the best. It gave me these beautiful mountains, serenity, and peace of mind. At least, until you showed up. And maybe even that has worked out for both of us. You, Jared the Seeker, have given me human contact again.

"Although you were a wet-behind-the-ears city kid, you brought communications back to me. You have caused me to re-think some things. And by the same token, you have learned much and have become a stronger person." Elijah quickly broke off his line of thinking and turned back to the present abruptly. "But that's enough jabbering for now. Here, drink this hot broth, then go back to sleep through the night. You should be about mended by tomorrow."

The Prophet was right again. A few days and he was well, stronger, and happier than ever. He felt he owed so much to this little man, and he had an idea. "Elijah, I need to help out more around here."

"You do fine, Jared the Seeker. You've chopped more wood than I need for two winters. You do your share of hunting, gardening, repairing the cabin, cooking."

"Let me go down to the village of Paradise and get supplies for you. I need to get out a bit on my own, if I am eventually to pursue my seeking. What say?"

They were sitting outside the cabin on a log, enjoying the first rays of the morning sun through the pines. The Prophet was quiet for a long time. "Okay. You are right," he said, finally. "It's a long trip. Takes a full day. Maybe the longest hike you've taken. But you are right. You need to spread your wings.

"First light of dawn, tomorrow morning, Dog can go with you to kind of look after you. You can take my big pack and I'll send some moccasins, buckskin gloves, and a few wood carvings you can trade to that ornery Harry Brock at the general store. He's honest, but bargain with him and get the best deal you can. Tell him you are my long, lost nephew or something like that. Get the usual: salt, sugar, flour, whatever you think we need." Then he added, "And get yourself some candy. Not good for your teeth, but it will remind you of what you have been missing," Elijah said, cackling.

CHAPTER FOURTEEN

It was a long hike, like Elijah said, and dusk when he and Dog headed up the familiar trail to the cabin. The pack on Jared's back felt like it weighed three hundred pounds. A couple of blisters had broken on his heels and were stinging from sweat. Dog barked his hello to the Prophet, who came out to greet them.

"I'll bet you know what tired is now," teased the old man as he lifted the pack from Jared's back and set it down near the door.

"Right you are. I am wiped out," Jared agreed breathlessly, beads of sweat standing out on his tan forehead and dripping down his cheeks.

"Dog take good care of you?"

"Sure did. He's a good companion." Jared stooped and ruffled the dog's fur. The animal wagged his fan-like golden tail in thanks. "By the way, Elijah, what kind of dog is Dog?"

"Well now, let's see. He's part golden Retriever, part collie, part Irish Setter, and part German Shepherd. That makes him the best purebred mongrel I've ever known. Right, Dog?" the old man said, chicken cackling.

Dog barked yes and Jared was sure he saw the animal smile, his lips rising over his great K-9 teeth, brown eyes twinkling.

"Come on in, you two. I've got roast turkey, hot soup, and my best home cooked bread waiting. There's a basin of water and towel for you to wash up first, Jared." He threw a meat-filled bone to Dog, who began to gnaw eagerly. "Make a good bargain with Harry Brock?" Elijah inquired.

"I think so. Can we wait until tomorrow to unpack?" Jared asked, chewing hungrily on a drumstick. "I'm ready to hit the sack after chow."

"Don't worry," Elijah pursued, "I can unload the stuff.

"No, wait 'til morning. I have a couple of surprises."

"Okay, suit yourself. It can wait," Elijah agreed with mild curiosity. "You hop into bed as soon as you finish eating. I'll sit out here on the doorstep with Dog and play you a lullaby. Made me a flute today."

Jared the Seeker went to sleep peacefully tired, listening to the enchanting music the old man played. He had never been happier.

The Seeker awakened stiff, but refreshed. He had even beat Elijah arising, stirred up hot coals in the fireplace, threw more wood on the fire, and put a pot to boil. Then, secretively, he rummaged in the pack and took out a plastic bag. He scooped out three handfuls of the ingredients, dropped them into the pot, and began stirring with a large wooden spoon. Then he reached with a free hand into the pack and took out a handful of something else and dropped it into the mix.

A few minutes later, the old man stirred and sat up, yawning and rubbing his good eye. "Up pretty early for a city kid, aren't you?"

"I am not a city kid anymore, even if I once was, as you seem to think," Jared answered boldly.

"I admit you've made progress. Smells good. What is it?" the old man asked as he dressed.

"One of the surprises I mentioned; oatmeal with raisins. I've mixed up some powdered milk in water to pour on it and honey to sweeten it."

"Getting fancy, aren't you? You'll get us both spoiled, if you don't watch out. Then we'll get soft and want more pleasures of life."

"It'll be good for us. We need a little pampering," stated the boy, smiling mischievously. "Besides, I was tired of that gruel, whatever it is, that you always mix up."

When they finished two bowls of oatmeal apiece, the old man looked at the boy with what might have been admiration gleaming in his eye. "Alright, I'll admit it," he concluded. "That was delicious, absolutely delicious. Brings back memories of my so-called civilized days."

Jared stood, facing the old man, smiling mysteriously. "Are you ready for the next surprise?" he asked.

"I supposed I had better be ready from the tone of your voice," Elijah answered, compliantly.

Jared fished in the backpack and held up a shiny, silver object. "Know what these are?" he asked, teasingly.

"Course I do," Elijah answered suspiciously. "They're scissors." He shivered and acted as though he didn't know why Jared had purchased them. "What in tarnation do we need them for?"

"We need them to give you a haircut, and I am the barber."

"Oh no you don't!" The old man rose from his box-chair, as though to run. "No way do I have my hair cut," he roared, indignantly.

"Well, I say you do," Jared retorted, grinning, holding the scissors in the air and threateningly opening and closing them with a click, click, click, the blades flashing in the sunlight through the window like killing knives. "I'm bigger and stronger now," Jared said, advancing toward the little old man. "I think I can whip you, if I have to. I intend to get the job done peacefully or otherwise."

"But I won't be a prophet without my hair," the old man protested defensively in a high pitched voice.

"Hair does not make the prophet," countered a determined young man. "It is the heart, mind, and spirit that makes a prophet. What is inside, not outside. A true prophet can be bald. Isn't that what you would tell me?" He stood over his beloved savior.

The old man went limp. He was defeated. He looked up at Jared and chuckled. "You win, my boy. You win," he said meekly, and sat down on his box-chair. "Go ahead with the deed. Cut away, as Shakespeare might have said."

The scissors snipped away; clip, clip, clip, to apprehensive silence from the victim.

Jared stepped back to admire his work. "Now a trim for the beard."

"That, too?" asked the Prophet, glumly.

"That, too." After what seemed like hours to the victim, but actually twenty minutes, the barber said, "Finished." The old man's hair now fit under his hat, and his beard was trimmed to only a foot long, tapering at the end, his mustache a clever upturn at the corners under his long, narrow nose. One could actually see his lips, which were full and congenial in what seemed a perpetual smile.

"Saints be blessed," muttered Elijah, feeling his head and beard with gnarled fingers. "I am naked with my hair all gone!"

"It isn't all gone," Jared protested. "I've just made you look half human again. Now I can distinguish you from the beasts." Jared joked, giggling.

"Very funny," mumbled the Prophet, but Jared sensed some pleasure in the old man's voice.

"How long since you had a haircut?" asked the Seeker.

"None of your business," Elijah answered, which Jared realized was his usual escape when he refused to divulge information or had nothing to say.

"I should have gotten a mirror, so you could see how decent you look. I might say even handsome!" he added, grinning, satisfied with his efforts.

"Heaven forbid!" replied Elijah, not as disgruntled as he pretended. "But I'll get even with you, watch and see."

CHAPTER FIFTEEN

The magic crept in overnight. He awakened before the old man and went to the creek to splash cold water on his face. As the sun broke free of the mountain, he looked up, gasped, and ran yelling back to the cabin. "Elijah, Elijah, come out! Get out here quick."

The Prophet staggered out the door, rubbing sleep from his eye. He slept wearing his hat and eye patch. "What is it, boy?"

"Look! Look everywhere; the colors, red, yellow, orange, gold, green. A rainbow of colors below, above, all around. The leaves have turned colors overnight! Never have I seen such beauty. Even as my other self, whoever I was. I know deep down inside that I have never experienced this wonder before."

The old man let out a deep, roaring laugh, much different from his usual cackle, expressing spontaneous joy. He was pleased to see the wonder in the boy's eyes; see that he had discovered one of the miracles of nature. "Awesome, marvelous, wonderful, incredible; all those things, isn't it!" he stated. "Autumn springs upon us overnight, unannounced, but it is really Indian summer, a time between summer and autumn. The days and nights are still warm. A chill hasn't come in the air, yet." Then he said more quietly, almost to himself. "Yes, sir, the Creator sure knew what he was doing when he made the seasons. We humans are almost ready for a change at the same time as Mother Earth."

He put his arm around the boy's shoulders and they walked over and sat down on the doorstep of the cabin to watch and drink it all in. It was more than could ever be done justice through words, written or spoken, or even through a painting or a photograph. "I am happy at the pleasure this discovery has given you, Jared the Seeker," said Elijah after a long silence of mutual thought and appreciation. "Now that you have experienced one of the joys I have, living here in the mountains. My paradise, my Utopia, my place in the sun."

"I think I could stay here with you forever, Elijah, and forget my other life and who I used to be."

The old man turned his face to Jared, voice quivering. "But it is not to be, my son. I see into your life and your journey to manhood. You were meant to be a seeker." He looked down at the ground, dejected. "The time has come for you to move on with your seeking. A few more days and you must leave..." This last nearly ripped out the old man's heart. He loved the boy.

"But I don't want to go, Elijah!" Tears leaked, overflowed, then ran down the boy's brown cheeks. He leaned his head on the Prophet's shoulder. "I feel like this is my home," he sobbed.

"I don't want you to leave, either. You have given me more joy and more to think about than anything that has happened to me during my many years in these mountains. But you are still a boy with much more to learn; much more to experience in your seeking. This I know." Then his voice changed. "But we have a few more days," he added, jovially, "and I have one more tough trial for you before I send you off. I told you I would get even for that haircut. I'll tell you about it later. Let's go hiking today and forget our worries and work. We'll hike without destination. Just enjoy the mountain trails. What say, Dog?" Dog barked eager agreement.

The next day, a bit stiff in body from their hike the day before, they sat on a log in front of the cabin, after a supper of cold turkey. "This is the plan, Jared," explained the old man. "You are going on your Vision Quest."

"Vision Quest, What is that?" asked Jared, not too eager.

"It is something I learned from my Indian friends in the Four Corners area. That's the only place in the United States of America where four states: Colorado, Utah, Arizona, and New Mexico meet at right angles.

"Anyway, a Vision Quest is a good thing. It is when a boy goes alone to the mountain, the highest peak in the area. He spends three days and three nights seeking his own personal vision. Finds out what it all means…the universe. It is when you must turn your seeking inward. On that mountain, you will think; you will contemplate, you will ponder, you will meditate. You will ask yourself the big questions. Where did you come from before arrival on this earth? Why are you here and what is your specific reason for being here? And where will you go after you go through the process of death and leave your body behind?"

He studied the boy intensely with his one eye to see if he understood. A very smart lad, he concluded. Very teachable; an excellent student. Eager to learn, hungering and thirsting after deeper meanings. Jared the Seeker stared back into the wise, old, blue-white eye as if to say, I'm listening. I understand. Go on. The Prophet continued, "There was a great lady I had the privilege of meeting many years ago, when I was a lad about your age. She made a lasting impression on me. She was deaf, blind, and had difficulty speaking. But when she spoke or wrote something, it had depth. Her name was Helen Keller. She could see and hear more with her spiritual eyes and ears than ten hearing and seeing people. She was, I believe, attuned to the infinite.

"Mid many of this fine lady's words of wisdom, she said, "The best and most beautiful things in the world cannot be seen, nor touched, but felt in the heart.' She, of course, was referring to spiritual and internal thoughts and concepts.

"Jared, my son, while you are on that highest mountain peak, the one you have seen up behind our cabin; while you are up there alone, learn to use your spiritual eyes and ears. To help you do this, you will fast for three days and nights. You will be allowed water, no food, to keep your system functioning. I will fill two canteens for you and there are clear creeks from which you may drink. You will find that your body shrinks and your spirit grows stronger. Questions?"

"What am I looking for? What am I supposed to learn?"

"We are improvising somewhat. Most Vision Quests are in the

spring, but that's okay. One thing you must discover is your own protective creature, a creature who is to be your guardian; a guardian spirit. The second is that you must stay awake to see the morning star. It will be a mystical moment when the moon is lowering in one half the sky and the sun is rising in the other. A magic moment few have really seen and pondered.

"You will rest and relax tomorrow and leave the following morning. This will be your final test, before I send you on your further seeking journey."

CHAPTER SIXTEEN

Jared made his way carefully up the mountain, taking in the beauty so never to forget it. Fat squirrels scurried off in front of him, cheeks stuffed and puffed out with nuts to store for winter. Mountain blue birds called warnings to one another that an alien approached. Chipmunks chattered excitedly.

He broke loose from the scrub oak and dense brush onto a plateau. Before him was a lake, shimmering brightly. It was smaller than the one below that they had swam and fished in, but just as beautiful. A stream of pure water from melting ice and snow ran into it from the mountain and another ran out, cascading downward. It came to him that he had seen no trash, no sign that humans had even occupied the area. Could it be possible that he had found a place where humans had never been?

He stretched out prone at the edge of the lake and drank deeply of the water, then sat up and looked around. The area was abundant with wildlife. He could see and hear it everywhere; the water, the creatures, the foliage, the sky; nature in conversation.

Elijah's last advice to him was a quote from Isaiah, Chapter Forty. It advised to walk in righteousness, seeking the eternal. He took his small Bible from his buckskin jacket. Yes, there it was. The Creator's promised to those who sought after the spiritual that He would…he read aloud, 'renew their strength; they shall mount up with wings of eagles; they shall run and not be weary; and they shall walk and not faint.'"

He closed the book, put it back in his pocket, pondered, and repeated, "they shall mount up with wings of eagles." Just as he said that a majestic Black Northern Bald Eagle, with a wingspan of eight feet, swooped down from the sky, claws extended, and crashed into the lake. The great bird emerged, its powerful claws clamped onto a huge Rainbow trout. The king of birds tried to rise with the ponderous fish, which was nearly as large as its cap-. tor, flapping its wings desperately. Jared feared the eagle would drown with the fish clamped in its long, sharp, curved talons. But it finally broke free of the water and became airborne, soaring overhead, the fish struggling uselessly, its fantail waggling and flashing in the sun.

The eagle lit with its prey, not ten yards from Jared, and began tearing the fish to pieces with its powerful hooked beak, then rose with its claws and beak full of fish flesh and flew up into a dead pine tree behind Jared. He followed it to its nest, where a mother and two, ugly, squawking eaglets waited hungrily to receive their meal in a huge nest made of sticks and brush,

Father eagle, known in ancient times for his power, courage, and majesty flew down again to the fish, and pranced proudly around, like a mighty warrior. He acknowledged the human, and spoke to the boy in his mind, glaring at him with glinting, wise eyes. "See what I do. I am a mighty eagle. I can provide for my family. I fear nothing, not even you, who are human."

Jared acknowledged that he understood and repeated, "They shall mount up with wings of eagles." It was then it became clear to him what the scripture was trying to express. He bid farewell to the eagles and began his climb again. He felt closely related to all living things, to the earth that we share and call home.

The peak, the pinnacle, the summit, whatever it might be called, was the place he would seek his Vision Quest. The wind blew freely, the air thinner. He breathed deeply, filling his lungs. He felt alive. There were mountain peaks, as far as he could see, most below him. Trees pulsated with the colors of autumn.

He chose his spot to meditate and seek his vision against a huge rock. He could climb on top of it and see in all directions. He took off his canteens and bedroll, all he had brought with him. Although it was what the Prophet called Indian summer, he had said it would also be cold during the nights at this altitude, near twelve thousand feet.

He scouted around and found a stream cascading from a small glacier down the east side of the mountain about fifty yards away from his camp. He drank from it, splashed water on his face, then looked up to see Great Horned Owl gazing down on him from a tree branch. Could it possibly be the Prophet's Owl that had followed him? It spoke inside his head. "You are learning well," it said. "And you will learn much more." And it flew away.

Back on the peak, he rolled out his blanket and sat upon it, watching the sun lower in the west. He felt at peace. Then his stomach growled, reminding him of his hunger. He quickly brushed thoughts of food from his mind.

Night came with its various sounds. Below, a wolf howled. He had never heard such a mournful sound. Far across several ravines another answered, its howl echoing through ancient canyons. Night birds called to one another, while small creatures scurried through the underbrush. The darkened world came alive, so different from the day. He was not afraid. Who could fear a universe made so beautiful for joy and experience by a loving Creator that Elijah had taught him about and of whom he was learning in his Bible.

The stars seemed to sing like angels. Every living thing hummed its unique song, blending together in a mighty symphony that entered his being and made him feel a part of it all.

CHAPTER SEVENTEEN

Elijah the Prophet paced nervously back and forth in his rustic log house, then outside and around the cabin. He gazed up toward the dark peak of the mountain. Dog paced with him, whining at his master's anxiety.

He muttered quietly, anguished, worried, as he paced. "Maybe it was premature. He might not have been ready. It's awful cold there this time of year. He kicked at the ground, threw down his precious hat and stomped it. "There are wild beasts up there! Maybe I am a senile old fool. No! I am a prophet. I know what is right. The boy is ready. He has learned much of the spirit within. His body has grown strong. He has broad shoulders, a muscular chest and powerful arms and legs. He survived the bear and the snake, and I know he has the blood of the American Indian in his veins.

"Yes, Jared the Seeker was ready. Well prepared. He will be all right. He will learn what the mountain has to teach him," Elijah told Dog in a low voice, as he picked up his hat, brushed it off, and slammed it back on his head. But he still paced, all night and the next two nights.

Jared awoke to the sunrays warming the rocks around him. He was wrapped tightly in his bedroll, and had slept in the center of a ring of boulders that formed a shelter from the wind. He sat up and stretched.

Morning came like a crescendo, another movement of the mighty symphony. Below him, massive pines, firs, and spruce soaked up the solar rays in towering dignity. The mountains invited him to join their banquet; a feast for eyes, laid out in sparkling splendor. He felt he had waited all his life for this moment, an unheralded instant of knowing. Somehow he had been meant to experience this. He kneeled and raised his face to the sun, and sang one of the sacred Indian songs the Prophet had taught him.

> The sun comes up
> The sun rises
> All is day
> It is enough to say
> It is day

Then he stood and raised his arms. "How old are these mountains?" he asked the sky. "Can a time be put upon them? Or are they above and beyond time? I think they are. And who put you there, Sky, to watch over everything? And there is wind. Why can it not be seen? Is it made of the same stuff as the spirit that is within us? He asked many questions. He pondered them, knowing they couldn't be answered to mortals, but savoring the questions and the pondering nevertheless.

Suddenly, he realized that he had fallen asleep and had not observed the morning star. He chastised himself. He felt hunger pangs, but went quickly down to the cold stream, drank deeply of the sweet water, then splashed some on his face. He felt good, inspired, thankful to be alive.

Throughout the day he enjoyed the constantly changing view. He thought about the old man who had sent him to this mountain. Was Elijah really a prophet or just an eccentric hermit? That question still bothered him. Prophets were from ancient times, weren't they? They were mighty men from the Bible. But he had experienced unexplained events. The Owl had spoken to him inside his head and led him to the old man's cabin, who expected him and knew Jared the Seeker; seemed to know too much about him. And how Elijah had enchanted the bear, Jared had understood what he said in the strange language. There were so many unexplained things. And the final mystery, who was he, Jared? Who was Elijah? Where did they come from? How did they get here in the mountains? It seemed they were destined to be together. Here, at this time.

He stretched out on his back, looking up at the endless, blue sky patterned with a few wispy cirrus clouds. He found himself entranced

by a huge, white thunderhead, called cumulonimbus that kept building higher and higher, spreading out and up, like white smoke pouring out of a tall smokestack. Still building, expanding, changing like an angry, erupting volcano. A tiny speck appeared on the outer edge, broke away, then fell through space. It grew larger as it dropped closer to Jared. But he saw it was not falling, but floating, and was in control. It came closer, and was a person, a beautiful woman, who landed on her feet in front of him, a translucent, green glow surrounding her.

"Who are you?" he asked, amazed.

"I think you know, Jared."

He drew a yellowed, timeworn photograph from his subconscious memory. It matched the woman standing in front of him. Stately, would describe her. Stately and beautiful. She wore a dark-green satin blouse and purple skirt that reached to the tops of her moccasined feet, her waist cinched with a silver studded belt. Her black hair was pulled back to a tight bun, held with a shell comb. Necklaces of colored stones hung around her neck. She looked at him with wide set, brown eyes, above high cheekbones. Her lips were straight, but curled up at the corners into a slight smile.

"You are my great-great-great-grandmother," he ventured.

"Just call me Lavinia," she said.

"You are...you are beautiful," he stammer shyly. "Are you Native American?

"Thank you for the flattery, you know how to win a woman over. Yes, I am Indian, as Columbus named us and it seems to have stuck - Cherokee; one of the smarter tribes. My man, your great-great-great-grandfather,a mountain man, is a fine fellow. We are still together."

"But you are so young, yet must be a couple of hundred years old."

"There is no time, as you know it, after you depart your earth life. Today, I was privileged to be one of the cloud people and drop down here because I have things to teach you and a message for you. Then I must return to my place in eternity."

She told him many things, old stories given to her by her own grandmothers with several greats in front of their names. Tales that went back to the very beginning, when the Great Plan was formulated by the gods and Grandfather Sky. She taught him many truths, then said, "I must go."

"Must you leave so soon? I would like to visit and get to know you," pleaded Jared, his brown eyes wide with wonder.

"I would like to visit also, my son, but I must leave. You will see me again when your earth journey is completed. I advise you to do as Elijah tells you. He is one of wisdom, though he does not fully realize his own power and wisdom yet. He will tell you to travel to the Four Corners area, the place in America where four states connect. There you will find Native Americans, as you call us. You will live with them for a spell and discover your past you are seeking. You will learn of your present, and have a window of choice opened to your future.

"Do I make myself clear? Do you understand my message?"

"Yes, I think so."

"Do not 'think' so, boy. Yes or no. Do you understand my message?"

"Yes, Grandmother."

"I said to call me Lavinia. Grandmother makes me sound so old," she said with mirth.

"Yes, Lavinia. And thank you for letting me see you."

"Thank you, Jared the Seeker, for calling me down. Your wavelengths summoned me. You are attuned. Remember to listen to the still, small voice, and it will lead you. Our goal as spiritual beings is eternal progression, which means learning never ends. Now I must go." Without another word, she began to rise into the sky, fading as she lifted higher and higher.

A loud clap of thunder startled Jared. He blinked his eyes, He was still lying on his back. Had he dozed and dreamed? Or was the vision real?

He found it difficult anymore to distinguish real from…from what? Imagined, dreamed, or subconscious? A passage Elijah had read from Shakespeare popped into his mind. It was something about our lives are but dreams and we are players and passing shadows in that dream.

The sun was lowering, and the thunderhead cloud had spread and turned black and ominous. A storm threatened. He must build a shelter. He went down to the tree line, gathered long sticks and boughs, and spread them over the boulders where he slept. He interwove them into several layers. They would not be completely waterproof, but would provide some protection.

Rain began just as he completed the shelter. The sky grew dark before night came. The rain fell steadily. Again, he would be disappointed. He would see no stars, let alone the morning star.

He had made a mattress of pine boughs, so rolled up in his bedroll, feeling hungry, lonely, and forlorn.

CHAPTER EIGHTEEN

He awakened to a gloomy gray dawn and peeked out of his bedroll. The atmosphere seemed strangely light. Then he saw it. Snow! About four inches of the white stuff. He crawled out of his bedroll, shivering to the bone. The snow had fallen down to about seven thousand feet. Below that, just rain. He shivered again. It was too cold to get up, so he crawled back into his warm blankets.

He lay drowsily and recalled that he had dreamed again of the beautiful house with fine furniture, a man, a wife, and two girls. He was part of the dream, was in the house, but not really part of the people. They treated him politely, like an alien a visiting stranger. He drifted into other dreams, and awakened much later.

Blinding light! He shielded his eyes as he looked out at a brilliant wonderland. The sky had cleared, the sun straight above, lighting up the snow that sparkled like diamonds. It was melting into miniature streams from the sun and warm wind. He scooped up a handful, put it in his mouth, and savored the cold as it melted in his throat. He no longer felt a need for food. His loneliness had fled. He enjoyed the solitude and knew the difference between the two. He would experience this day in awareness.

That afternoon as he sat upon dry boughs he had dragged out of his shelter, he smelled the damp earth, the rotting bark, the eons of decayed matter that the wetness of the snow had renewed, the fresh odor of pine trees sown below. His senses were keen.

But his thoughts were broken by the sudden awareness that eyes were watching him He heard clucking, chirping all around him. The clucking chatter came from the tree line below. A long line of pine hens were moving up the mountain in procession, and gathering around him in a circle, perching on bushes and rocks on the ground.

Elijah had told him about these strange birds. Many had never seen humans. They were gray, brown, black, and white in their feathers, with red combs around their eyes and heads; a cross between grouse and wild turkeys. He must remember to find out the scientific classification of these creatures called pine hens. There surely must be pine roosters. Why were they just called hens?

Dozens of the birds surrounded him, blinking lazily at him, curiously. How and why had they suddenly appeared? Where had so many come from? He had seen none on his way up. They did not appear to be afraid; they were more curious, even friendly.

They moved closer to this human creature. He reached out to touch one. It shyly moved back, but did not leave. Jared's audience again started clucking and gurgling, which he began to understand inside his head, much like he understood the Prophet's owl. "Speak to us," they said. "Tell us of many things that we need to hear."

He felt foolish at first. What do you say to an audience of birds? Then it occurred to him that he might tell them stories his great-great-great grandmother had related to him during her visit. She had taught him about the birds and animals that were present from the beginning of the Earth Plan, when all creatures talked and mingled together.

The pine hens clucked anxiously begging him to speak. He began rather self-consciously. "I am Jared the Seeker. I am here on this mountain as part of my training for my seeking."

He relaxed and started to enjoy this experience. "I will talk to you today, my friends, about some truths that my great-great-great grandmother taught me about your kind and many of your brothers and sisters. The stories were passed down to her by her grandmothers. They go back to the beginning and the marvelous mother of us all: Mother Earth."

The pine hens blinked their eyes, nodded their heads, and

clucked agreement to the words that touched upon familiar things from their past.

"Mother Earth was created first," continued Jared, encouraged by the interest of his audience. "She is the mother of all living things that dwell upon her. In turn, other things were created in their order, all in their due time and pattern. Next, came Father Sky with his sun, moon, and stars to give us light by day and guidance by night, and bring about tides upon the oceans, seasons, wind, and all kinds of weather. Then came the waters, rain, and mist from heaven, the oceans, seas, lakes, and rivers. These elements working together, according to the Plan of the Creator, caused growth of green plants, trees, fruits, vegetables, and colored flowers. Finally, upon Mother Earth, came the creatures. These were the masterpieces of the Creator: walkers, flyers, swimmers, crawlers, and creepers.

"Last to be created was the two legs; people. Because they were last they were the youngest of creations. Therefore they had to be taught by other living things, who were older and wiser."

The birds clucked and nodded excitedly. Some fluffed their feathers, flapped their wings. One shouted inside Jared's head. "Yes, yes, our own ancestors told us these stories. They were passed down and are familiar to us. They are true stories, but they have become vague in our memories. We need to hear them again."

Jared was thrilled at the response from his enthused audience, who did not seem to be in a hurry to leave. He had completely lost his self- consciousness and forgotten the difference between bird and human.

"I am happy that you also have these vague memories. During the visit with my ancestor, she spoke of those forgotten times when we were brothers and sisters, communicating with one another in thought and purpose; learning from one another. All living things respected Mother Earth back then…"

BOOM! BOOM! BANG! BANG!

Gunshots, then the hurried, frightened sound of four feet racing through the trees and brush below. It was deer hunting season. Crazy, disrespectful hunters were in the mountains, men who killed creatures just for the sport of it. The pine hens looked at one another nervously, eyes wide in fear. They began to disperse, some flying up into the pines, but most waddling off awkwardly, like little people. Gone as mysteriously as they had appeared. It was silent. A chilling breeze blew around the boy. He was alone, sitting in the fading sunlight, wondering if this day had really happened. Reality or illusion?

CHAPTER NINETEEN

The third night descended upon his mountain. He had begun to think of it as his mountain because he felt its pulse and heard its breathing, slept upon its breast at night and felt its heartbeat. The sunset was beautiful and beyond description, changing from gold to pink to peach, and rose. With tears in his eyes, he began to sing an ancient Indian song, one the Prophet often sang, in the tongue of a people long gone, as though it was his own language.

> Night birds sing to the sky
> Songs of love to the red sky
> It is not day
> It is not night
> The time is suspended between
> A time for singing

The sky turned gray then black velvet. Millions of stars appeared. Had anyone ever attempted to count them? They surrounded him in an endless dome of sky. They danced in and out, farther, closer. He felt he could reach out and touch them. Some appeared to be below him and his mountain. He felt he had floated off into space, observing himself below. There was a presence of ancient spirits, humans, and creatures. They hummed softly to him, giving him courage to stay alert this night and fulfill his mission to observe the morning star.

He sat cross-legged upon a large boulder. Almost in a trance, he waited, chanting old songs that came to him from out of somewhere.

Suddenly, it appeared on the horizon. The Morning Star! It

still shone brightly as others faded with the first light of dawn. He continued to watch, spellbound by the star that lingered alone, peer to no other. At that moment, an overwhelming peace enshrouded him. His heart sang and his lips and voice followed.

It is a time of joy
Peace fills my being
My eyes see clearly forever
My ears hear every sound
A new strength fills me
Happiness walks with me
I am surrounded by beauty

He finished the song and a large butterfly lit on his wrist. He lifted it up before his face. It was yellow with black trim designs and a row of blue dots. Time stood still. Its wings slowly opened and closed, and boy and butterfly observed each other.

Jared suddenly realized that it was beyond the season for butterflies, the altitude too high, the weather too cold. It was too early in the morning for butterflies to be out. Yet here was one, perched on his wrist. After several magic moments, it fluttered off and disappeared. This was an omen meant only for him, the fulfillment of his Vision Quest.

Sunrays began to light the sky, though it had not yet shone on his face. Jared the Seeker had learned the lessons of the mountain. It was time to start down.

CHAPTER TWENTY

Dog heard him, smelled him. The Setter tore wildly out of the cabin and saw him hiking down from way up on the mountain. He raced up the trail toward the boy, yelping and barking a happy welcome. Jared caught the dog as he leaped into his arms, knocking him down and sending him sprawling. They rolled joyfully on the steep trail, wrestling, tumbling over and over.

By the time they reached the cabin, Elijah had made a pot of hot vegetable soup, with big chunks of potatoes, carrots, and venison. Bread was baking. He hugged the boy, relieved to have him safely back.

"Sit down at the table, Jared the Seeker, and we will eat and talk." He spooned out two large bowls of the steaming soup and poured each a tin cup full of cider. "Eat slowly now, you hear. I know your stomach must be touching your backbone. But you have to recondition your insides to food gradually, or you'll heave it all up." He bent to pour Dog some cider ina bowl and gave him a venison bone. Dog lapped up the liquid, then lay at Jared's feet contentedly chewing on the bone.

They ate in silence for several minutes, until the Prophet wiped his mouth with his sleeve. "Tell me, was your Vision Quest successful?"

"It was. I think I learned what the mountain had to teach me. I felt things…changing me…things in my mind…inside me" He searched for words. "It was like my spirit was moving inside me and I could feel it…The real me. Then like it left me and I floated out a ways, observing my body. Do you know what I mean, Elijah? Am I making sense?"

The old man looked at him with understanding in his one

eye. "Oh yes. Yes. I do know what you are saying. It is good, the things you have learned. You have realized in three days and nights what few people learn in a lifetime, the lessons of the spirit; lessons that can't be learned in books. They have to be felt in the heart." The Prophet licked his lips anxiously. "And did you discover your guardian creature?"

Jared hesitated. "I did."

"What is to be your guardian creature?" he asked, curiously.

Jared looked down at the table and stated quietly, "A butter-fly."

"A butterfly? A butterfly?" he repeated, half muttering to himself. "Just like a city kid. I thought you might have discovered it to be a wolf, a bear, a cougar, or an eagle. But a butterfly? Are you sure you didn't misread your omen?"

"I am sure. It is to be a butterfly. Not just any butterfly, but a big one. It has yellow wings with a black border. Blue dots on the bottom of the wings."

"A Tiger Swallowtail," stated the old man with renewed interest. "Go on. Tell me the rest."

Jared related the incident when the butterfly lit on his wrist at the moment he saw the morning star. He told of every detail, trying to express his feelings of that moment.

"It is good. Forgive me for judging so quickly, my boy. It was meant to be and you were receptive. A butterfly is to be your guardian creature. Look to it for messages from the still, small voice that will speak to you in your mind whenever the Swallow-tail butterfly appears to you, whether in reality or in dream or vision."

They were quiet. Dog nuzzled Jared's leg for another pat. "Tell me, Elijah the Prophet." Jared had begun thinking of the old man as a Prophet, "Tell me, what is your guardian creature?"

"None of your business," snapped the old man, changing his demeanor abruptly.

"I told you my whole story. Why won't you tell me yours?"

"Because I am the Prophet and you are the Seeker. There s no need for you to know. A seeker is a student and will learn when the time is right."

"Is it that owl that led me here," Jared persisted. "It shows up everywhere."

"No, the owl is just a messenger, a friend that hangs around. Now forget it. Someday you might find out. For now, we have work to do; preparations to make. We will all swim together in the lake tomorrow for one last time. You, me, and Dog. The following day, you must leave here to continue your seeking."

This news caught Jared like a blow to the chin. He had not thought about leaving. He had settled here comfortably and begun thinking of this cabin in the mountains as home. "But I don't want to leave. I like it here. Why can't I stay?" he protested hotly.

The old man's composure slumped, sagged like a pile of rags. His head drooped low on his chest. "I don't want you to leave, either, " he replied quietly. "You have given my life new purpose. I wish you could stay, but winters are harsh here and it is coming. Sometimes I am snowed in the cabin for weeks, until I can shovel out or a thaw comes."

"But I could help," Jared interrupted.

"Indeed you could. I am not saying you are incapable. You have grown strong. You are a much different boy than the lad who first staggered to my cabin door. But your destiny is not to be found here and now. You have learned all I can teach you. Maybe someday, in the future..." His voice trailed off. Then he spoke again with finality. "It is to be. Tomorrow, we swim in the lake. You will leave the day after tomorrow, and continue on your journey. Remember, you are Jared the Seeker.

CHAPTER TWENTY-ONE

The lake was trimmed in a delicate, crocheted pattern of ice and the mountains wore ice caps all around them. Jared looked at the water hesitantly, but saw the old man tearing off his clothes, so he followed suit. Elijah, Jared, and Dog dashed into the icy water like three children playing chicken. They splashed wildly only a few seconds, then backed out. Dog shook off crystal drops while Jared and Elijah shook uncontrollably. They wrapped themselves in blanket towels. Gradually, their shivering stopped, and with the help of the sun, their blood began to warm and circulate.

"Makes you know you're still alive, doesn't it?" said the Prophet, teeth still chattering.

"Or makes you wish you'd die and go to a warmer place," replied Jared, laughingly.

"One more time in to remind us how good life is," dared the old man.

"I don't know if I can do it. Look, my skin is turning blue."

"We can dance around more vigorously after this dip. Let me tell you something, my boy. This is what you will remember long after you've left these mountains. You will think about bear, the snake, and this cold dip in the lake. See, I made another poem for you." He cackled his chicken laugh. "Yes, sir, I promise you it is the rough times, the adversaries of life that make us strong and we remember the longest. Let's go for it. Last one in eats worms!"

The boy did not know how he survived the icy water. Back in the cabin he felt warmer, more at peace. There was warmth inside him. Silently, they ate hot stew, warm bread, and steaming cider, which they shared with Dog. They sat on the doorstep, watching the late autumn sun go down.

"The days are much shorter now. The sun goes down early and we'll do the same," said the Prophet, breaking into thoughts. "Before we hit the sack, being as I am a prophet, I will give you a blessing."

"What is a blessing?"

"Well, it's kind of a pronouncement upon your head that beseeches the Great One to send his angels to watch over you, and give you certain characteristics you might need. Follow me?"

"Not really."

"You will. It'll come to you gradually, as all blessings must. Come inside. Sit on the chair." Dog curled up by the boy's feet, looking up at him seriously. "Now I place my hands upon your head so that powers from above know I am acting in the capacity of a prophet. The powers will come from above through me, into your arms and out of my hands into your head and being."

On this rare occasion, Elijah removed his pointed hat, and ran his fingers through his hair. He bowed his head, taking on his prophet's demeanor, then placed his hands on the boy's head. "By the powers that be," he began, "I bless you with courage and discernment." He broke the spell to lean over Jared's shoulder. "Do you know what discernment is?" he asked.

"Not really."

"It means you will have the ability to read people, see behind their eyes and lips. To look beneath the surface of their skins and see their hearts and minds, to tell lies from truths, to know those who are sincere and could become your friends. The great god above has already blessed you with the power to speak and understand the languages of people and creatures."

The Prophet slipped back into his prophetic self and pronounced many blessings upon Jared the Seeker. Then he paused to think, and said, "Being as I am a prophet, I must prophesy in your behalf. That's what a prophet does best."

He ran his tongue around his lips, raised his face up as though looking through the cabin roof to heaven, then lowered his head again, and continued. "You, Jared the Seeker, must go to the place called the Four Corners, where Arizona, Utah, Colorado, and New Mexico meet. There you must seek out the Native Americans, as you call them. It is the place where there is the largest gathering of Indians in America. There you will find a temporary home. And there, after you have learned much about those people, you will find your other identity, the Jared you once were."

The Prophet seemed disturbed, agitated. He removed his hands from the boy's head. Jared started to stand. "No!" shouted the old man. "I am not through prophesying. I was not going to continue, but I must."

Jared sat down again, somewhat confused at Elijah's behavior. The Prophet placed his hands on the boy's head again. He was silent, struggling within himself for sometime before he could continue. He started shakily. "You will discover your former identity. You will reunite with your family, but things will not be the same. You will struggle with anxiety and dissatisfaction. You will be forced to make a serious decision that will change the course of your life." He paused, then added, "Amen."

"What does amen mean?

"It means the end. It means that I am through blessing and prophesying. And it means, hopefully, that it will come true. It means, literally, so be it. Now let's get some sleep. Tomorrow is a big day."

CHAPTER TWENTY-TWO

The Prophet was up early while the world was still dark. He had prepared a special breakfast: oatmeal topped with fresh raspberries that had been preserved in jars in the creek, pancakes, fried venison, and hot cider. He prodded Jared awake. "The big day, my boy. Be up and about."

"Mmmmm, smells good," said Jared, as he pulled on his buckskin pants and jacket.

"Eat plenty. This may be your last home cooked meal for some time."

When they went to the creek to wash their dishes, gray dawn was distinguishing the mountains from the sky. Back in the cabin, the old man told him, "I've got your backpack ready to go. The big one. I put in a bedroll, a canteen of cider, lots of dried jerky, fruits, and nuts. Your money is in the little side pocket, along with your watch. Keep the Bible and pocket knife in your jacket."

Jared unsnapped the side pocket and took out the silver watch. "Here, I want you to have this. I know you don't need time here in the mountains, but wind it every night and think of me."

Elijah rubbed its silver surface with his thumb and turned it over in his hand. "It is inscribed and a very valuable old pocket watch. Are you sure you want to part with it?"

"Yep, I won't need it. I can tell time like you do now."

"Thank you, my boy. I don't have much to give you, but what my hands have made." He went to a shelf. "Here is a belt I made from the snake skin, the one that bit you, and I have woven the rattles onto a beaded necklace." He slipped it over the boy's head.

"They are beautiful, Elijah. I will remember you always. And thank you for taking me in all these months and teaching me so much."

"You have taught me, also, Jared the Seeker. One more thing…" He handed Jared an envelope. "This is a note to a friend of mine, name of Al Varner. He is a truck driver with Rocky Mountain Trucking in Denver. I have written his name and address on the envelope. Give it to him and he will see that you get to Four Corners. Make your way first down to Paradise, and the storekeeper might be able to get you a ride for a ways. Denver is many miles, but you've got nothing but time in your favor. Got it?"

"Yes, I understand."

They stood awkwardly, looking at each other, then grabbed one another in a bear hug. Jared wasn't sure, but he thought he saw a tear fall from the old man's' eye and trickle into his whiskers. Dog whined pitifully, as he sensed the parting. Jared kneeled, ruffled his fur, hugged the huge dog and held him close while Dog licked his face.

"Two bits of parting advice," said the old man, moistening his lips with his tongue. "The first from our friend Shakespeare: 'readiness is all.' The second is the mighty Apostle Paul's wisdom to his friend, Timothy, in his second epistle" 'God hath not given us the spirit of fear; but of power, and of love, and of sound mind.'

The boy's eyes blurred as he shouldered his pack. Daylight was arriving as he started down the trail. He did not look back. Elijah the Prophet and Jared the Seeker parted. The only sound one could hear on the morning air was Dog's mournful wail.

PART TWO

EXPERIENCE

CHAPTER
TWENTY-THREE

It was daylight, with bright sunshine. The boy saw Great Horned
Owl following him down the mountain trail, flying from tree to
tree. Owls were night birds, but then, of course, this had to be a
special owl. A messenger, the Prophet had said.

Jared broke out of the tall pines onto the lower foothills. A
message came to him out of the wind and into his mind from owl.
"Remember the things you have learned. Remember the teachings of the Prophet."

He judged by the sun that it was afternoon, maybe two o'clock
as he trudged wearily into the small settlement of Paradise. The
storekeeper remembered him and treated him to a cold root beer
and Snicker candy bar, then talked a young married couple, both
dressed in jeans and plaid shirts, into giving the boy a ride to the
next town. They were from back east and seemed reluctant, but
consented under urging from the storekeeper. Jared threw his pack
into the back seat of the expensive car and crawled in beside it.

The man, a blond, athletic type, turned from his driving, asking, "Been with the boy Scouts?"

Jared was confused. "Er...uh...no."

"I thought with the buckskin outfit and all, that you might
have been on a Daniel Boone hike with the scouts."

"Oh, no. I...I've been living on the mountain. With a friend."

The man and woman exchanged glances. The woman, also
blond, hair coifed in a short bob, and very delicate, with nails
polished blood red, asked suspiciously, "Then you don't go to
school?"

Jared searched quickly for an answer. " I used to, but schools are too far away from where I lived. My uncle has been teaching me."

They drove through farm and cattle country, mid surrounding mountains. Jared noticed the couple kept sniffing and turning up their noses. They whispered and glanced at him. He found to his amazement that he not only could hear their whispers quite clearly, but could discern their thoughts. He remembered that the Prophet had blessed him with discernment. He understood that the couple thought he stunk and was dirty. They did not want him with them.

Finally, the driver stopped the car and turned to Jared. "Better use the restroom. We might not pass another for awhile."

Jared went inside and to the restroom, and when he came out the couple and the car was gone.

The sun had fallen below this part of the world. The sky darkened with a covering of black clouds. A storm was approaching. It hit almost with his thought. Snowflakes fell thick and heavy. The wind blew. It was a blizzard. There was a barn to his left. He climbed a high stone fence and crossed a field toward it. It was warm inside. His eyes adjusted to see several cows, a horse or two, and some hay stray. He dropped his pack, tired, and snuggled into some straw, covering himself with its warmth, and slept.

"Wake up! Get out of here!" a voice shrieked in his head. He was suddenly alert. Above him, on a rafter, glaring down, were the yellow eyes of an owl. "Get out of this barn and off this land. Run. Now!" warned the owl.

Without hesitation, he shouldered his pack and raced out into the cold night. The wind had stopped, but snow still fell. A dog was barking in the distance. A man shouted. "Stop, thief! Stop or I'll shoot."

Jared ran, panting with exertion, his pack bouncing awkwardly on his back. Boom! Buckshot sprinkled his pack. The dog was gaining, barking, snarling. He ran faster. The fence. His first leap failed. He fell back in the snow. He got up and with full effort on the second leap, made it over to the other side into a dry ditch, just as the dog hit the fence, snarling viciously, teeth bared. He got up and ran down the dirt road, putting space between himself and the unfriendly farm. Sweating, panting, he dropped under a huge tree, out of the snow.

"What did I learn?" he asked himself, out of breath, then answered his own question." That there are good people and bad people, and there are good dogs and bad dogs."

He rested. Caught his breath. He was hungry. He took off his pack and opened it for his canteen and piece of jerky. But his hand felt something big. He pulled it out. In the dim snow light he made out the Shakespeare book. The Prophet had given him his precious book. Tears came to his eyes. He was alone in the cold night, and he missed the strange little man who had taken him into his warm cabin and heart. He swigged from the canteen and chewed the jerky, feeling sad and sorry for himself. He had no family; no friends.

He saw headlights coming down the road. A motor car? No, a truck; a big truck. Headlights shone high off the ground. He would chance it for a ride. He quickly closed his pack and stepped out onto the side of the road. The huge, maroon eighteen-wheeler slowed and stopped before he even stuck out his thumb. The passenger side window rolled down. "Climb up in the cab! It's cold with this window down," shouted the driver as he swung the door open.

Jared threw his pack up onto the seat and climbed in. The fat, hairy-armed driver threw the pack in the back to the sleeping compartment. It was nice and warm in the cab. "Camping season is over," said the driver, laughing, his vast stomach jumping up and down. "Don't you know it's winter?"

"So I've noticed. Caught me off guard," said the boy, teeth chattering.

"Any particular place you're headed?" the trucker queried, curious about this boy in buckskins, out on a winter night in the vast, cold country.

"I'm going to Denver to look up Al Varner at Rocky Mountain Trucking."

"Good news and bad news," the driver said with good humor, his voice grating and nearly as deep as the diesel engine in his truck. "Good news is that you are riding in a Rocky Mountain truck and Al Varner is my best friend. Bad news is that Big Al is on a long haul up through Montana into Canada and clear up to Alaska on the Al-Can highway. Be gone three weeks, a month, maybe longer; depends on his loads. I can drop you off near the YMCA. You can get a bed and meal there. Maybe you can find work and hang around, until Al gets back. How's that sound?"

"Good. I'm in no hurry. I sure am glad you came along. I had…I had kind of lost my bearings a little. I didn't quite know what to do."

The trucker asked no awkward questions. They rode quietly for several miles, then he broke the silence. "We're off the beaten path here. Back roads. I like to break the pattern now and then; get off the freeways and out of traffic. There's a little country town up ahead. Nice home cooking type restaurant. Bet you could use a hot drink and a meal."

"I can pay for our meal," offered Jared.

"Nope. This one's on me. Happy to treat a friend of Al's. By the way, my name's Bill."

CHAPTER TWENTY-FOUR

"You were right, Bill," commented Jared as they walked out of the diner. "Best food I've eaten in along time; steak, eggs, hash browns."

"That hot cocoa warm you up a bit?" asked the jolly truck driver, smiling.

"Sure did. I thank you for the meal."

"Not much traffic comes along this road, so the old couple that runs the place make food extra special for folks who stop. They get up any time day or night and cook for hungry travelers."

The moon faced, bald, pot bellied trucker eyed Jared, appraising him. "I know you're tired. It shows. So crawl up behind the seat, in the sleeper, and sack out. There's a pillow and blanket back there. I'll wake you when we get to Denver.

It seemed to Jared that he had just closed his eyes when he was shook awake by a pudgy paw, calloused from many miles at the steering wheel. "Better get up and see the big city of Denver, gem of the Rockies. Any place special you want me to drop you at?"

Jared sat up and rubbed his sleepy eyes. "No. No place special. I'll find a place to stay, something to do, until Al gets back."

"Okay, I'll let you off at the next corner. Go straight down that street two blocks, turn right two blocks, and you'll find the YMCA. They might put you up. If they're full, turn around and go in the opposite direction a few blocks and you'll find Saint Paul's Christian Center. They will be good for a meal and bed."

Jared pulled out his pack as the truck stopped near the curb. "Thank you for your kindness. I don't know what I would have done if you hadn't stopped for me."

The trucker waved and pulled away. Alone again. He didn't like big cities. Too much cement, not enough nature. Gray, smoke-filled sky, with no sun. He guessed it was afternoon, maybe two or three o'clock. He slipped his pack straps over his shoulders and started down the sidewalk through the snow, slush, and cold. Two blocks down, he turned right. Several rough looking boys, dressed in blue jeans and leathers stood across the street on the corner. They were bigger and older than him, and spotted him. "Look, it's Daniel Boone," shouted one," his long hair flying in the cold winds..

"I think it's Davy Crockett, King of the Wild Frontier!" yelled another.

"I guess he's Kit Carson!"

"Let's take him and see if he's got beaver pelts or gold in his pack!"

They started toward him, mean and full of trouble. He picked up his pace, then broke into a run. So did they. His pack made it awkward to run. Try to lose them, he decided. Hide. He cut into an alley. This was a wrong decision. It was a dead end. He dropped his pack at the end of the alley and turned to face them. There were four of them. The first made a lunge for his pack, Jared kicked him in the shin and socked him in the face with his closed fist. The attacker went down. The second swung at him and missed. Jared kneed him in the groin and smacked him in the nose. Blood flew. Then one of them caught him with a blow to the side of his head, knocking him against a brick building. Another blow closed his right eye and he went down on the cold, snowy pavement. How do you prepare to be beat to a pulp, he wondered fearfully. But no more blows came. Then he heard a deep voice. "Unfair! Four against one. Try me, cowards."

Jared squinted up with is good eye and saw a muscular, powerful black man dressed in only red gym shorts, his bare torso shining in the cold. Two bullies rushed him and he cuffed them aside like flies, his great arms spread like eagle's wings. Then he grabbed the other two by their long hair in his enormous fists, lifted them off the ground like a black Samson, banged their heads together hard, then dropped them like rag dolls. He addressed the other two in a deep, base voice that vibrated in his thundering chest. "Now pick up those creeps and drag them out of here before I squish you all like the nasty bugs that you are!"

He leaned down to speak to Jared. "You hurt, son?" he asked, concerned.

"No, sir, just my pride, I suppose. I figure I didn't have to fight nice against four of them. Like no rules."

"You did just right. I looked out my window and thought you might need some help. I live upstairs in an apartment. Come on up and let me fix that eye."

"Thanks. I appreciate your help," said Jared, picking up his pack and following the great, black giant.

In the kitchen of his richly decorated bachelor apartment, the black man dabbed at Jared's swelling eye with a ball of cotton soaked in alcohol. "My name is Leonard Steam. My teammates and fans call me the Steamroller. I was pumping iron in my work-out room when I saw you below in the alley."

"Pumping iron?"

"Yeah. Lifting weights; barbell, dumbells. Got to stay in shape. I'm pro football, Denver Broncos. Fullback. When they need a few years for a first down, they give it to the Steamroller. I've gone over for six points with three, four guys hanging on me.

"You a runaway, Jared? Not that it's any of my business. I ran away about a dozen times when I was a kid."

"No...er...I don't think so," said Jared, hesitantly.

"What do you mean, you don't think so?"

Jared discerned that he could trust this kindly giant, so he told him his story, at least most of it. When he finished, Steam appraised him for awhile in silence. Then he said, "Sounds like a fairy tale to me. You say you been livin' with an old hermit in the mountains? He wasn't a pervert, was he? I mean...you know. Did he make you do strange things and...?"

"Oh no! Nothing like that. He was kind of weird, eccentric

and all that, but he saved my life more than once. He taught me
lots of things about nature and life. He read to me from the Bible
and Shakespeare. In fact, he gave me his book of Shakespeare. There
in my pack." Then Jared added as an afterthought, "And he became my friend."

"Been livin' that long in the mountains, huh," said Steam,
half aloud. "There was an airplane crash up there somewhere, several months ago. But there were no survivors."

Airplane crash! Flashes seared into Jared's mind. Screeching
steel. Shattering glass. Pine trees. Screaming. Then nothing.
Leonard Steam was still talking when his mind returned.

"You want I should put your picture on a milk carton," he
ventured.

"I don't understand. What do you mean?"

"They put missing kids pictures on milk cartons with a phone
number to call. Everyone drinks milk, see. So one day your mama
goes to pour some milk for breakfast and she sees your picture, and
says, 'Oh Lordy, there's my little baby Jared.' And she calls the
number and finds her missing kid and happily ever after."

"No. Thanks anyway, Leonard, but I feel I have to find my old
self in my own way. Maybe there's more for me to learn in my
search. Elijah, my mountain friend said for me to look up this Al
at Rocky Mountain Trucking. He gave me a note to give to him
with some instructions in it. So I'll wait until he gets back."

"Okay," agreed Steam, shrugging his massive shoulders. "You
got anywhere to go? Anywhere to stay until Al gets back?"

"Not really."

"Then you're staying here with Steamroller. I need company.
You'll have to sleep on the couch. "I'll only fit in my special bed,
made for my extra big body."

"Great. I can pay you rent. I've got a little money."

"No way. Don't insult me. I make more money than a hundred people in a lifetime. Tell you what, Jared, you stink like an
NFL locker room after a close game. Get out of those duds and
into that hot shower there. Towels are on the shelf. While you get

yourself cleaned up, I'll take those mountain buckskins to a leather cleaner and pick up some civilized clothes for you. There's a store I know just a couple of blocks from here. Let me see your feet so I can judge your shoe size. And here's your own key while you are my guest. I'll put it here on the table. Now hit that shower."

CHAPTER TWENTY-FIVE

Leonard Steam returned with an armful of clothes in boxes and bags and dumped them on the kitchen table, just as Jared came out of the shower with a towel wrapped around his waist. "You fall in love with that shower?" Steam asked, laughing, his great white smile spreading across his face from cheek to cheek.

"It was great! I don't remember having one so wonderful…I don't remember having one at all!"

Leonard's huge chocolate eyes widened as he noticed three white scars that stretched from Jared's shoulder to elbow. "Them stripes where the bear got you?" he asked amazed.

"That's right," answered Jared, fingering the scars.

"And that thing hangin' around your neck belong to the snake?"

"Yep. His rattles; eight buttons. That means he was a pretty big one. Diamondback rattlesnake."

"Maybe your story is not a fairy tale after all," concluded Steam, thoughtfully. "Here's some duds for you. Get into them nice jockey shirts. Make you feel human again. And here's a T-shirt, socks, and the best pair of Nike cross-trainers out! Jeans, sweatshirt, jacket." He walked into another room and returned with a ball cap. "And to top it off, here is an official Denver Broncos ball cap to keep your head warm. Speaking of head, you got long hair. You want to get a haircut?"

"No thanks just the same, but I'm on my way to Four Corners to look up some Indian friends of the Prophet, and Indians mostly wear long hair, he says. So maybe I'll fit in."

"Suit yourself. Your head, your hair. Leonard slumped into a huge leather chair while Jared dressed. "You be kind of brown yourself. Got some Indian blood in you?"

"A grandmother with several greats before her name. Full blooded Cherokee," replied Jared, proudly as he pulled on the jeans. "You guessed my size right, Leonard! You sure you won't let me pay? I feel like a taker."

"Nope. Don't need your money, don't want it. Makes me feel good to help out. I got so much money it makes me feel sinful and guilty. I could never spend it all. Bought my mama a nice house back in 'Bama. Hepped my brother and sister get educations. They most all be educated, 'cept old Leonard here. There be ten of them. Couple doctors, a lawyer, chemists, teachers, nurse. My daddy took off a few years back. Fatherin' got to be too much for him, I suppose. But mama stuck with us and worked mighty hard."

Leonard paused and chuckled, his even, white teeth shining in his dark face. "I be the least educated and make more spendin' cash than all my brothers and sister put together. But I learned there be a lot more to livin' than makin' money. I got picked up for football right out of high school. An exception in the NFL. I suppose some rules were bent. But they wanted the Steamroller and offered me plenty, so I took 'em up on the offer. Mama was disappointed I didn't go to college. But she still love me and, grateful for me heppin' out the family. You tired of listenin'?"

"Not at all. You heard me out on my story. Eleven kids. Wow! And it's hard for me to imagine so much money, as you say you made. I don't know much about money. I woke up in the mountains and had quite a bit in my pocket though. And you make that much playing football? Tell me more."

Leonard laughed deep in his barrel chest. "You a good listener, Jared. I'll be glad to have you around." Then he got serious again. "I'm not pure black myself. I imagine they're not too many pure left of any kind of people. My mama told me we had a white grand daddy way back in the family. He owned some of my tribe as slaves. She told me lots of my grand folks was slaves. Lived terrible hard lives back then."

Leonard Steam was quiet for awhile, watching Jared try on his

Nike shoes. "These shoes are so comfortable, I can hardly tell I have them on," said Jared, looking his thanks at his benefactor.

"Thought you'd like 'em. Those you were wearing were nearly worn out."

"Yes, I had them when I first met Elijah. He made me sandals for the summer, and I put these back on when I left. They're a bit tight now. I guess I've grown." Jared was amazed at this giant black man who had taken him in. He wanted to know more about his world. "I'll bet your family, your mama, your brothers and sisters, are proud of you, a football hero making lots of money. Famous. Will I get to see you play?"

"Sure. I'll take you to our home game this weekend...I'm a slave in a way," he stated pensively.

"You're kidding."

"Nope. Listen up and I'll explain. See, I'm bought, just like the old-time slaves. Only difference is I'm a millionaire slave. I get paid for being a slave. But I'm bought, just the same. The owners of the team, the big bosses, buy my body and I must produce, or they trade or sell me to another team. I mostly got nothin' to say 'bout it. Bought and sold, like slaves. They buy all of us that play the game. Don't get me wrong. I love money. But even more I love the game, the sweat, the pain, the competition."

Jared could sense the excitement when Leonard Steam spoke about "the game." It shone in his eyes, in his heavy-jawed face, and posture.

"I can run a four-five," he continued. "I can carry four guys on my back. I can sprint, dodge, shift, hit, hit, hit. Keep my feet churning, even when I'm going down. And let me tell you, boy, that as much as myself and my teammates love the game, the bottom line is win, win, win! If we start to lose too often, the fans quit coming. Fans are fickle people. And then the money for the team owners drops off. If I weaken and don't or can't do my job, fill my assignment, then I'm traded, and somewhere down the road I'm cast off and become a has-been, a nobody."

He was breathing heavily, living in his world of football. Then suddenly relaxed. "But like I say. I'm not complaining for now. Slave or no slave, it gives me life. But enough about old Steamroller. Back to you, Jared, who christened himself The Seeker. You say you woke up in the mountains with your memory gone?"

"Yes, sir, that's it. I don't know who I am, where I came from, how old I am. Nothing.""

"Well, as to your age, I've had enough brothers to judge you are about thirteen, fourteen, maybe fifteen. I'll say thirteen or fourteen. You got some muscles developing. While you're with me, I'll teach you to pump iron and define those muscles. You all dressed and feeling human now? Well, let's go get us some grub. I never knew a boy who wasn't hungry. I know the best eating place in the territory; called Aunt Ellie and Uncle Elmer's."

CHAPTER TWENTY-SIX

The garage was on the other side of the building, which was under tight security. Although it was not in what could be called a ritzy section of the city, it was luxury, with comfort only money could buy. There were studios, artists, musicians, bankers, and athletes like Leonard Steam.

"This is Jared, a guest of mine, Alex," said Steamroller, introducing the boy to the gray haired garage security man. "He will be with me a few weeks, maybe more. So give him the same rights as me. Okay?"

"Sure thing, Leonard. If you need anything, Jared, just let me know."

When they came to Steam's parking stall, Jared's jaw dropped open. He stared at what looked like a shining red car out of a science fiction story, with gray leather upholstery and trimmed out in chrome from front to back.

"Like it?" Steam asked, grinning.

"Wow! Gollee. I've never seen anything like it."

"It's the one toy I allow myself. Don't care for fancy clothes or gold jewelry, like a lot of my black Brother. But this toy, I like. Maserati; Italian sport. Candy apple red. Had it customized to fit my extra large body, the driver's seat moved clear into the rear so's I can slip in easy like. Hop in and we'll cruise out of here in style."

Steamroller steered the car confidently through the city streets, while the boy from the mountains took in all the sights, eyes wide with curiosity. "Leonard, by the way, how big are you?" he questioned.

"Glad you asked, my friend," said the giant man, smiling at the boy, teeth glistening with health. "I'm six feet eight inches tall, weighing in most times at around two hundred ninety seven pounds." Then he added, with a grin, "Solid steel muscle, of course."

Both laughed, enjoying one another's company.

After another period of silence, Leonard said, quietly, "Wish my brain equaled my body."

"Your brain seems plenty above average to me," Jared said. "Tell you what. You can teach me pumping iron stuff and I'll brief you on some Shakespeare, so you can impress your teammates."

"You got yourself a deal, man."

Steam turned down a dimly lit street and pulled in at the end. There were several cars parked around a well- lighted building with a green and blue blinking sign. "Here we be. Ellie and Elmer's Place. Come on in and meet some mighty fine folks."

The place was rustic, wood, with old-fashioned red and white checkered tableclothes, rattan chairs, and filled with smiling, congenial people. As soon as Steam's frame filled the doorway, people rushed to greet him. "Look who's here, the Steamroller!"

"Come on, join us, Steam."

"Yeah, man, come in and have good food and good company, Leonard."

"This here is my friend, Jared," Leonard Steam informed them, his arm around Jared's shoulders.

"You get yourself in a lot of trouble, hangin' with the Steamroller," a voice retorted from the crowd. All laughed.

"If he is trouble, then I've been through the worst of it before I met him," Jared replied, laughing.

"You got yourself a loyal brother there, Steam."

"Let me take him into the kitchen first and meet him up with the folks who turn out the heavenly food," stated Leonard, chuckling. "Then we come back and join you to eat and talk."

He led Jared into a spacious stainless steel kitchen where a half dozen people were busy with hot ovens, sizzling grills, and pots boiling with good smelling foods. "Elmer and Ellie, take a minute off to meet my friend."

A small, bird-sized woman and a tall, skinny man came forward, both blacks wearing white aprons over day clothes; him in jeans and denim shirt and her in a flowered house dress. They looked to be in their seventies. "This here is my new friend, Jared. He wandered in from the mountains. Jared, this underfed couple are Elmer and Ellie. They own this place. They also responsible for the food of paradise, of which we are about to partake."

Elmer shook hands with Jared and Ellie hugged him to her frail frame. "You be wonderin' why we both so underfed. It because this giant Steamroller eat us out, and we left with just a few scraps," she joked, laughing and toothless.

"I offered to get her some nice pearly white choppers, so she could eat properly," said Leonard. "But she said she want nothin' false on her real self. Ellie, think you can find work, a job for this boy?"

"You know how to work, boy?" she asked bluntly, wiping her bird claw hands on her apron.

"That I do know how to do," assured Jared.

"Then there be a job for you. We got dishes, pots, pans, utensils, to wash forever. Think you be comfortable bein' around us black folks? Our color go from tan to brown to black, but we all be African Americans."

Jared had not noticed until now that they were all blacks. "Won't bother me, ma'am, if it doesn't bother anyone else. Besides, I'm kinda brown myself," he observed proudly.

"Want to start tomorrow?" she asked doubtfully.

"You bet."

"Okay. You be here seven in the mornin'. We start you at minimum wage and feed you lunch."

"I'll drop him off in the mornins' on my way to the stadium," offered Leonard, "and pick him up in the afternoons. I'll buy our dinners here. Don't like to cook myself. If I'm not here before dark, put him in a taxi. I'll take care of the tabs."

"You want your usual grub tonight, Steam?" asked Elmer.

"Why not. When you get a winner, stick with it, I always say. Start the boy with a small serving. See if he be an eater first."

Jared and Steam returned to the dining area and joined some other folks at one of the large round tables. Jared felt good. Relaxed. These were happy people and they included him in their talk. The food came and Jared's eyes popped. "You call mine a small size? I've never seen this much food," he exclaimed, amazed.

"You take care of that and there be more, if you want it," Leonard said, kindly.

The dinner was made up of a huge steak, golden baked rolls, mashed potatoes smothered in gravy, carrots, peas, cauliflower, and broccoli, with plenty of hot cocoa or cold milk. Dessert followed – apple pie with vanilla ice cream.

On the ride back to the apartment, Jared commented, "Never, ever, have I eaten such delicious food. And so much. You'll have to roll me upstairs." He looked at his benefactor gratefully. "I thought I could eat a lot, but you ate three times more. Amazing."

"I'm three times bigger than you," said Leonard Steam, grinning. "And you know, I thinkin'. How you know you never seen a car like mine or eat like that before? Maybe you be from a rich family or somethin'."

Jared had completely forgotten that he was the Seeker and that he had another life. "You might be right, Leonard. I had completely forgotten. Tonight...today has been so much fun. I had forgotten that I don't know who I am or where I belong." He became quiet, trying to think, trying to remember.

"I'm sorry," apologized Steam. "I shouldn't have reminded you. Shouldn't have brought it up."

"No. That's okay. I've got to think about it. I've got to face it and try to remember so many things. But how? Anyway, thank you, Leonard, for a wonderful day. I can never repay you for your kindness."

"You are welcome. It gives me pleasure to see a boy eat and enjoy it. And don't ever mention repay. You don't repay friendship with money. It is just there to be.

CHAPTER
TWENTY-SEVEN

Leonard Steam, alias The Steamroller, awakened to the sound of muffled sobbing. He kicked the blankets from his giant sized bed and staggered, bleary eyed into the living room, where he turned on a small table lamp and knelt down beside the couch where the boy was curled up facing the backrest. "What's the matter, boy, missing your mama"" asked the black giant kindly.

"The boy turned over, facing him. "Sorry I woke you up," he sobbed.

"No problem. I'm a light sleeper, anyway."

Jared sat up and rubbed the back of his hand across his tear stained eyes. "No, it's not that. I don't know what I'm missing. Just missing myself, I guess. Who I used to be, or should be. I just feel like an alien, like I don't belong anywhere."

"Maybe you wouldn't like who you used to be. Maybe you wouldn't like your old life," Leonard empathized.

"Maybe. The Prophet, old Elijah, hinted at the same thing. But I have to find out for myself. They grew quiet. A radio played soft music from somewhere out there in the night. Someone coughed. Sound carried far in an otherwise silent city. "We've been reading Shakespeare, you know, and I just remembered a line that comes nearest to how I feel. Would you hand me the book there by the lamp? I'll see if I can find it. You don't mind too much? I mean me being a boob and all," Jared asked, embarrassed.

"Not at all. I'm glad you got me acquainted with that Shakespeare fellah. He sure seems to understand us humans, our problems and all." He handed the big book to Jared. They listened to the wall clock humming away the seconds that turned to minutes, while the Seeker flipped through the pages, Steam sitting on the floor, looking at him, like a child waiting for its mother to speak.

"Here it is. I found it. This is from 'The Comedy of Errors.' Antiphalus of Syracuse is speaking: 'Am I in earth, in heaven, or in hell? Sleeping or waking, mad, or well-advised?'" He closed the book. "That's the closest I can explain to what I feel. Get the picture?"

"I believe I do," said Steamroller, sympathetically. "Think you can get back to sleep now? Think you'll be okay?"

"Yeah, sure. Thanks, Leonard, for listening. Thanks for putting up with me."

"That's what buddies are for, man. Now stretch out and get some winks. Remember, you're going to the big Bronco game Saturday to see your hero, The Steamroller, mow down some opponents and win the game."

Jared turned over toward the back of the couch, while his friend rose and pulled the blanket over him, then stumbled back to his giant bed.

Football, Jared thought, is a game that is difficult to appreciate, more difficult to enjoy, if you don't understand it. Two lines of giant men facing each other, waiting to pulverize one another, trying to kill the one person with the ball. Somehow, he understood the game. Flashbacks entered his mind. Little kids playing the same game. He seemed to be one of them. His past. Where was it? What had happened to the past he had experienced and once knew?

He sat in a large, glassed structure atop an enormous stadium shaped like a bowl, watching the Denver Broncos, the Steamroller's team, and his friend. He was being treated with respect, like royalty because he was Steamroller's friend. Leonard Steam was someone to everyone in this stadium. Jared knew his number was 25. Someone handed him powerful binoculars and he saw each player, like he was next to them. He watched the expressions on their faces, the look in their eyes, their lips moving. What were they saying to one another?

Someone pushed a plate of steak, shrimp, and french fries in front of him, along with a big gulp root beer. Everyone spoke kindly to him and were friendly, like he belonged, all because he was Steamroller's friend. How had fate brought him to such a man?

He watched his friend score three touchdowns, carrying three or four opponents, who tried to bring him down, just like Leonard had told him. What power!

After the game, he was escorted to the Bronco's locker room by two policemen. Giant, muscular, sweaty men were laughing, slapping each other. High-fives. Leonard put his big, sweaty arm around Jared's shoulders, took him around, and introduced him to each of his teammates. He was overwhelmed with all the attention.

"You and me, we're going out to celebrate another win. Let's go to Aunt Ellie and Uncle Elmer's and see if their food is still the best in Denver," suggested Leonard, laughing. "You won't even have to wash dishes."

Aunt Ellie and Uncle Elmer's Place was alive with laughter, loud talking, and joking, as always. Leonard Steam and Jared were greeted warmly. Everyone was happy with another bronco victory and the part played by their hero, The Steamroller. Aunt Ellie came out of the kitchen to greet them as they sat at a table reserved for them. "You want this here boy to cook your meal tonight?"

"What you mean?" asked Steamroller, mystified.

"This boy Jared. This friend of yours. He be our number one assistant cook. He been promoted. "

"Why didn't you tell me, Jared?" roared Leonard, clapping him on the back with his giant, long fingered hand. "You know Elmer and Ellie never before let anyone else into their kitchen, and now they made you assistant cook. Let me tell you that is a real honor. Where you learn to cook food?"

"The Prophet," said Jared shyly. "I told you, me and him, we took turns cooking. He taught me a lot."

Leonard turned to Ellie. "I think he'll pass up cookin' tonight. We're out to celebrate, so if you and Uncle Elmer will hash up your A-1 best dinner, we'll promise to eat it like hungry bears and be grateful to you."

On the way home, Leonard remarked, happily, "Ah man, it's good to be alive. Tomorrow is Sunday. We both got the day off. We can sleep in late, then you can read me some more from that Shakespeare fellah's book and that little Bible that you carry around."

CHAPTER
TWENTY-EIGHT

"O, she doth teach the torches to burn bright!
It seems she hangs upon the cheek of night
As a rich jewel in an Ethiop's ear;
Beauty too rich for use, for earth too dear!
So shows a snowy dove trooping with crows.
As yonder lady o'er her fellows shows.
The measure done, I'll watch her place of stand
And, touching hers, make blessed my rude hand
Did my heart love till now? Forswear it, sight!
For I ne'er saw true beauty till this night."

"That's from 'Romeo and Juliet,'" said Jared, closing the book. "It's Romeo describing his feelings when he sees Juliet for the first time."

"Wow!" said Leonard. "What great language. That Shakespeare fellah sure knows how to put things. If I could talk like that I could have any a sweet chick I wanted."

"I'll bet you could have any girl you wanted now, without the fancy talk. You're a football hero. They would fall at your feet."

The giant man looked at the floor. "Naw," he said quietly.

"Why not? Haven't you had a special girl friend?"

"Well, I been out with lots…just for fun, good time and all, you know." He paused, looking sadder. "Mostly the wrong kind. Just party girls. Out with me because I'm famous or have money." He paused again. "There be one special one back in 'Bama. We went to high school together. I ought to forget all this life I'm livin' now and go back and grab her, if she is still available."

They had finished a late breakfast, which Jared had cooked, amazed at how much food his giant friend could put away. It kept him cooking for a hour, but he loved it. Leonard had eaten a dozen pancakes, half dozen eggs, half pound of bacon, half a loaf of toasted bread, a pint of orange juice, and a quart of Hot chocolate. They continued to sip the chocolate as they lounged and chatted in the living room. The weather was gray and cold and they felt lazy and comfortable.

"Read me that bit from your Bible again, about how you decided to become a seeker," suggested Leonard, changing the subject.

"Well, the book just kind of opened to that page in the bible," said Jared. 'And that particular scripture seemed to jump right out at me. Like there was some reason or purpose to it. In James, it was, but I've since found similar ones in other places. He thumbed through his small Bible. "Here it is. The same thing in Luke, Eleven – Nineteen. 'Seek, and ye shall find; knock, and it shall be opened to you.'

"That little line gives a lot to ponder," said Leonard Steam, as if pondering himself. "And that's when you decided to become a seeker and wandered into the cabin of the old guy, who calls himself a prophet. That how it came about?"

"That's about it. That scripture kind of gave me courage. Like a shot in the arm, you know."

"Incredible. Just incredible," said the big man, half to himself.

The wind howled and rattled the windows. Both were quiet in thought, listening. Finally, Leonard said, "Storm blowin' in. Maybe a wild Colorado gale, right out of the Rockies."

Jared had been thinking and gave voice to his troubled thoughts. "Leonard, I've called Al Varner at the truck firm three times. Twice he wasn't back from up north. The third time he had been sent out quick, like on another haul. You know, I have a good job. I could get me an apartment and just stay in this area. Seems as good a place as any."

"You welcome to stay right here with me as long as I'm with

the Broncos," offered his friend. Then he added quickly, "But then you wouldn't be a seeker."

Jared looked up quickly into the big man's black solemn eyes. "What do you think, Leonard? The Prophet said I should go to Four Corners and find the Indians, and there I would find myself. What do you think?"

The Steamroller was silent a long time as the wind howled louder and louder. "Hand me that Shakespeare fellah's book. I been readin' that since you introduced me to him. Seems he was someone who understands us humans pretty good. If I can find the part, "I'll give you an answer that isn't an answer."

Jared handed him the large book. He thumbed through the pages a long time, seeming to grow frustrated. Then his eyes brightened. "Here it is. I found it, believe it or not. Maybe some book learnin's rubbin' off on me. This that I'm goin' to read is a character named Portia, speaking in this play called 'The Merchant of Venice.'"

He began reading haltingly. "'If to do were as easy as to know what were good to do, chapels had been churches and poor men's cottages princes' palaces, it is a good devine that follows his own instruction; I can easier teach twenty what were good to be done, than to be one of twenty to follow mine own teaching.'" He closed the book and looked hard at Jared. "So what I'm tellin' you myself, my friend, is that I can't tell you what to do. No one can. This is for you and you alone to decide. It's your life and your decision. Know what I'm sayin'?"

The boy's shoulders slumped. His feelings, through his eyes, looked hurt. But he recovered, and said, "You're right, Leonard. Thank you. You are a good friend." Then he added, "And you are getting pretty good at Shakespeare, too."

Both laughed.

"I'll give it another couple of weeks or more and call Al Varner again. The Prophet never steered me wrong and had his reasons and foresight for wanting me to visit the Indian reservation. I think I'll keep on being a Seeker."

CHAPTER TWENTY-NINE

It was a melancholy Monday. The gray outside had turned to white. The storm had hit a fury, blowing wildly, stacking up huge drifts of snow, then settling into steady, fluffy flakes, falling, covering the world in a purifying white blanket.

Football practice was called off. Restaurants, stores, and businesses closed. Traffic stopped. The mechanical, technical, social, economic world came to a halt. There was stillness everywhere. The Steamroller threw his feet over the side of his giant bed. After three phone calls had disrupted his sleep, he decided to give up. He pulled a curtain aside and looked out, mumbling half aloud. "No goin' outside for a couple of days, at least."

He yawned and stumbled into the living room, where Jared was still snoring on the couch. "Better get yourself up, Jared the Seeker. You be the first in the shower and I'll fix us some breakfast. I'm not as good a cook as you, but I'll manage to get us some kind of grub. Then, since we been exercising our minds a great deal, we goin' to exercise our bodies today, while the snow covers up the world."

The workout room was spacious to accommodate the Steamroller's big frame. It contained the most up to date state of the art exercise equipment. There was everything imaginable for every part of the human anatomy. But Steam sought out the barbell and the dumb bells. "My favorites," he stated. "In my opinion, you are not pumping iron, so to speak, unless you're using a barbell or dumb bells. I was using them when we first met. Remember?"

"How could I forget! You saved me from that wild bunch."

"You were doing okay. Now I know you been workin' out in here pretty regular, but I got to give you some proper instruction that might help you throughout your natural life."

He picked up the barbell in one hand like it was a mop stick.

"Now a young fellah like yourself don't need to work for bulk. You got a pretty good body goin' along, as it is. Don't want to ruin it. What you need to be workin' on is definition. That means you just got to polish up your muscles a bit. Round them out. Firm them up. Define them. You start with lighter weights and few repetitions. That way, you won't hurt yourself. Got it?"

"Yes. So far."

"Okay. Now watch carefully. Lesson one is how to pick up the barbell." He set it down. Then he squatted, placing his hands shoulder length wide on the bar, fingers forward, thumb underneath. "See how I keep my back straight. Lift it now with the legs, not the back. Now I demonstrate the clean and jerk. Bring the barbell from your waist up to your chest, turning your hands over quickly, so they are holding the bar. Rest, balance, then split your legs as you thrust the arms and the weight straight up over your head. Bring it down through the steps."

He put the barbell back down on the floor. "I only showed you that because weight lifters do that one. We don't need to be weight lifters. I'll show you some of the major muscles you can work on. Your chest is called the pectoralis major. Your shoulders have the deltoid muscles. Your biceps are your front upper arm. Your triceps, the back upper arm. Your thighs are the quadriceps.

"Later on, I'll show you exercises you can do for each particular part of your body, but that is enough for you to go it alone for now. Oh yeah, one important muscle I should mention is the glutious maximus. That's your rear end. And you don't sit comfortably too much on that muscle or you'll never develop the others."

Both laughed.

"Golly, Leonard," said Jared. "You could teach a physiology class in high school or college."

"Probably could, but they couldn't pay me what football does. I've thought about teaching or coaching when I get older and my bod gets tired and worn down. Course I'd have to go to college; get me a degree. But maybe I'll just do it someday. Now let's get with it and pump some iron."

CHAPTER THIRTY

Jared reached Al Varner after two more weeks of attempts. The Steamroller drove them to meet the trucker, in his Maserati, at the Rocky Mountain Trucking Company. They introduced themselves while standing on the busy loading dock. When Jared mentioned Elijah, Al Varner, a look-a-like for an overweight John Wayne the actor, rough and ready, like many long haul truckers, but not nearly as big as Steamroller, became alert.

Jared handed him the envelope and a smile spread across the trucker's face when he read the note, which he stuffed back in the envelope and deposited in his jacket pocket. "So you lived with Elijah Worthington for some time?" he asked with a kindly western drawl. "I wondered what happened to him and where he disappeared to these many years. Yes, Jared the Seeker; that's what he called you in the note, you got yourself a ride down near Four Corners; that's where he said you are to go. I owe Elijah much more than one little favor like that."

"I never knew his name was Worthington," said Jared. "Somehow, I never even thought he had a last name."

"Oh, yes, Professor Elijah Worthington, a special person. I knew him well, or I thought I knew him.

"We got a long ride together, so I'll tell you what I know about him and you can tell me what you know." He turned and smiled at the huge black man, who everyone in Colorado knew as their football hero. "Can your friend, Steamroller, have you out at the rest stop on the highway south of Denver? Say one week from today at eight in the morning? We're not supposed to take passengers, that's why I have to meet you out there."

"Sure, I'll have him there," said Leonard Steam. "I know the place. I really hate to lose my buddy, but he feels he got to move on," Steam said sadly, gently squeezing Jared's shoulder in his big fist.

"Okay. From there I'll take you south, Jared, and we'll drive through some pretty country, through Durango, Mancos, Cortez, and Dove creek, then on to Monticello, Utah, where I'll have to drop you off. I'll then have to head north to Salt Lake City. You'll head south. You might want to study a map in the meantime to get yourself oriented."

All shook hands and departed.

They arrived early at the appointed rest stop and were sitting in Steamroller's car watching the long fingers of sunlight stretch from over the mountains down into the lower realms, illuminating rivulets of melting snow that still clung to the earth. Spring was rapidly moving into the area. Sprouts of green could be seen poking out of the black soil.

"I thought I'd be staying with you a few days," said Jared, breaking the silence. "And it turned into months. Seems like I've known you all my life, Leonard."

"Well, you have known me most of your present life. Me and that Prophet fellah you stayed with." He choked up and coughed a couple of times. "I'll miss you, Jared the Seeker. You have been a good companion. I hope you can get your memory back and find out who you used to be, and whatever else you might be seeking. And I thank you for teaching me things in your Bible and for introducing me to Shakespeare."

"I have more that I can tell you; more than I can ever thank you for, Leonard. You saved my life probably; took me in when you didn't know beans about me. Keep making more touchdowns and winning games," he added.

"Sure hope I can…I bet this is Al coming. An eighteen wheeler." He turned to Jared. "You got your pack, food, a couple of canteens of water? Need any money? I got more than I can ever spend." Jared shook his head in refusal.

The big black truck with silver trailer pulled up beside them.

Al waved. Jared gave Leonard Steam a quick hug as tears filled his eyes. Then he hefted his pack and threw it up through the door of the truck that Al had opened for him. Sad, but anxious to get on the road, he waved a final goodbye to his friend.

"Take care of yourself, Jared the Seeker," Leonard Steam shouted, as the growling truck pulled away, drowning his words. Sadly, eyes blurred with threatening tears, he watched it slowly disappear down the highway, until the back of the eighteen wheeler shrunk to a small speck on a thin ribbon of asphalt. Then he turned the car around and drove back toward Denver and his lonely apartment, where for days he would find signs of Jared's existence with him for so long; a lump in his throat when he saw the empty couch each morning where Jared had slept. He had grown to love the kid. Maybe someday he would see him again, but he doubted it. They were from two very different worlds.

Al spoke first as the truck pulled out onto the highway. "That Steamroller seemed like a fine fellow for such a famous guy."

"He was," said Jared, choking up again.

Al noticed and became silent, respecting the boy's privacy, as the truck hummed over the miles of road. They passed through peaceful country landscapes. And pastoral cattle land, then began climbing into mountains, green with pines, spruce, cedars, the patterns broken with patches of melting snow turning into sparkling streams cascading down ravines and gullies.

Jared had regained his composure and broke the silence. "So you knew Elijah?"

"Yep. Knew him well, or so I thought."

"You called him Professor Worthington. What does that mean?"

Al smiled at the boy. "It means he was a teacher; a professor at the university in English Literature."

"Oh, that explains his knowledge of Shakespeare. He gave me his book; the complete works of Shakespeare." Jared hesitated before his next comment, not sure he should make it, but went ahead. "He sure didn't seem like a college professor. I mean he didn't look like what I would picture one to be." He paused again, but decided to plow on into what might be forbidden areas. "He called himself a prophet, said he was Elijah the Prophet. He acted weird sometimes. Then other times he seemed real. He did things that maybe a Prophet might do. He saved my life a couple of times in ways hard to explain." He looked over at Al and asked the question that gnawed at him. "Do you think he was a prophet?"

The big trucker looked at him severely, yet questionably. He was quiet a long time and Jared feared he might have offended him or asked a forbidden question. But finally, Al Varner spoke quietly, almost reverently. "He can call himself whatever he wants, as far as I'm concerned, but to me he is a guardian angel. He saved my life – literally. I've never spoken of it to anyone but my wife, but since you know him in a different way, I'm going to tell you my story and the Elijah I knew."

Al Varner paused to collect his thoughts. "I was an alcoholic. A no good drunken bum. I lost my job and was losing my family and everything and everyone I loved. I was as low as you can get. I even thought of suicide. One night, after I had drunk myself to oblivion, can't remember much about it, don't know how I even got there, but I was passed out, laying in the gutter on skid row, in my own vomit and filth. Pukin' all over myself."

He paused again and Jared could tell it was painful for Al to speak of this part of his life. "Well, there I was," he began again, shifting gears on a hill. "There, in the gutter, a filthy, no good, rotten , stinkin' thing. And along came this angel in the form of a little strange guy named Elijah Worthington. He reached down, lifted me up a little, and slapped me half awake. I don't know how such a little guy did it, but he got me to his apartment, cleaned me up in the shower, bought me a set of clothes, filled me up with coffee, then, when I was reasonably sober, he cooked me bacon and eggs and pancakes.

"He talked to me all the while. Didn't preach at me or anything like that, just talked. He told me I had a family that's worryin' about me and needs me. Don't know how he knew that. He made me stay in his apartment a few days to think things over, then convinced me to join AA; Alcoholics Anonymous.

Al Varner looked over at the boy and smiled with relief that he had told his story. Then added, happily, "And here I am now, part owner of a trucking firm. Got a boy about your age, two beautiful daughters and a wife that must be an angel herself to have stuck with me through it all. So you see how much I owe Elijah Worthington? And come to think of it, maybe he is a prophet, just maybe he is. Who am I to say?"

"Wow!" exclaimed Jared. "What a story. That's sure a part of Elijah I never knew. He never would talk about his past. By the way, Al, how did he lose his eye?" This question had eaten at Jared. He hoped for an answer, finally.

"Trying to help people, just like he helped me. He spent most of his off time from the university trying to help drunks and homeless people. One day, he leaned down to lift up some wino, a guy with the D.T's, delirium tremors from alcohol, who was seeing snakes, bugs, and monsters, his mind about gone from the booze. Well, he leaned down to this guy and the wino reared up with a knife in his hand and stabbed the professor in the eye. An inch deeper and it would have killed him.

"That's when he disappeared. His eye had started to heal and the docs were talking to him about a false eye to fit his socket, but he just took off from the hospital. He didn't clear out his desk at the university or his belongings from his apartment. Nothing. Just disappeared. I figured he got disillusioned with humanity. And then you showed up with a letter from him after these many years. Tell me your story and what is Elijah like now?"

CHAPTER THIRTY-ONE

Jared wondered where to start, how much he should tell the big truck driver. But since Al had revealed so much about his painful past, he figured he could tell him most anything. Thinking about it made it seem so unreal. Many times he had thought it was a bad dream from which he would soon awaken. And he knew that talking about his experience would make it sound even more like a fairy tale. But what did he have to lose? The Steamroller had accepted his story. So he began, but left out the part about waking up in a pine tree; that just seemed too far out. "I woke up in the mountains," he began. "The first thing that hit me like a bucket of cold water, was that I didn't know who I was. Nothing. A big blank. I had some money in my pocket, a watch, and in my shirt pocket a little Bible. I still carry it there. Inside, written in ink, it said Jared. I figured that must be my name. I flipped open some pages to a part that said. 'seek and ye shall find.' So I thought, okay, I'll seek. And I called myself Jared the Seeker."

Al listened attentively, not interrupting, as Jared unfolded the story of how he stumbled onto Elijah's cabin. He left out the part about owl and thought even now that maybe he had imagined it. When he got to the bear story, he unbuttoned his shirt and showed Al the scars.

"Incredible," remarked Al. "You know the strange words Elijah used to send the bear off could have come from some of the natives he knew. He did study cultures and languages. He spent his summers with the Indians down where you are going. In his letter to me, he wanted you to locate some of his Indian friends. He felt it was important that you do. He hinted that you might, perhaps, find what you are seeking there in Navajoland. They call it Dinetah and call themselves Dine, which means The People."

Al geared down the truck. They were coming out of the mountains. A small town lay ahead in the valley. "I'm hungry," said Al. "I told you I could never repay Elijah Worthington, and you being his friend are the same to me as he. This trip will take me a day out of my way, but I own the company, so who cares?"

They had full bellies after a good meal at the café, felt comfortable, and were back on the road, traveling through more picturesque Colorado country.

"Tell me more about old Elijah," said Al after miles of silence. "It's been several years since he disappeared. What's he like now?"

"Well, I'll tell you one thing. You would never know he was once a college professor. At least I wouldn't," began Jared. He paused a moment. "Except now that I do know, it makes sense. His language when he recited Shakespeare was eloquent. It was wonderful watching his excitement when he performed, acted out parts, like he was actually each different character. And when he read from the Bible his voice took on a reverent tone.

"But, Al, you wouldn't recognize other sides of him. Sometimes he was real eccentric, weird acting. I thought he was just a crazy old hermit during those times. When he reminded me often that he was Elijah the Prophet, he was a different person again. He spoke with authority and seemed like a mystical guru. Some things he did seemed…well, like beyond explanation.

"Then the way he lived. He said he built the cabin himself. He grows a garden, hunts, lives mostly off the land. He has Dog for a friend and talks to it like it's human. He wears old clothes, a big loose coat. And he always has on this hat with the crown pinched up into a point and a black leather patch over his eye, like a pirate. He's all hair, down past his shoulders, with a beard to his belly. I forced him to cut his hair and trim his beard," Jared finished, remembering the day fondly.

"Nope, I wouldn't recognize him as the Elijah I knew," cut in the driver.

"But I have to tell you, Al," emphasized Jared, "that if I described his character and my relationship to him in two words, it would be friend and teacher. He taught me so much. He opened up my mind to think and question. I think he hated to see me go, but he sent me on my way because winter was soon coming and he thought it would be too hard for me."

Both fell into a prolonged thought about this strange little man, Elijah Worthington, who now called himself Elijah the Prophet. The miles and time passed by, until suddenly it was night, the truck headlights cutting through the thick blackness, following the yellow ribbon in the middle of the long, endless highway.

"I'm tired, Jared the Seeker," Al Varner said, yawning. "I'd better pull over at a rest area and we can both catch some shuteye. You can have the sleeper behind us and I'll stretch out here in front."

Jared did not hear the truck start up, nor was he aware of the many miles they had covered. When he finally blinked his eyes open, gray dawn had lightened the sky. He sat up, feeling stiff but rested, climbed between the seats, and flopped beside Al.

"Have a good sleep?" asked his friend, as he expertly steered the great truck along the black asphalt.

"Boy, I must have. How long have we been moving?"

"Oh, a few hours. We'll be coming into Monticello, Utah in a few minutes. That's where our trails part. I go north and you go south. We'll have breakfast at a café and pick up more grub to stuff in your pack. Sure hope you wake up or come around to whatever it takes to remember your past and who you are."

He ate well, not knowing when he might have such a good meal again. He pulled his pack out of the truck and slipped his arms into the straps.

"Just ahead, down the road, the next towns are Blanding, then Bluff. Get onto Highway 666 farther down. You can hitch some rides till you get clear down to open country and the reservation. Take a little detour and see the Four Corners Monument. That's where the four states meet. You can step your feet in Utah, Colorado, Arizona, and New Mexico. You'll see a different landscape than you have ever seen, I think. Good luck to you, Jared the Seeker." They shook hands and parted, the great truck turning to go on to Salt Lake City.

The morning was brisk, the sky clear, the sun lighting up this part of the world as Jared began his trek down the highway.

CHAPTER THIRTY-TWO

Alone, Once again on his own.

He hitched rides with two different truckers. Each knew Big Al Varner and thought him a great guy. Then he rode in the back of a beat up pickup with a bunch of Indians. No, they had not heard of Elijah. They said they were city Indians, that Jared would have to go farther south to find the reservation. They dropped him off in the middle of nowhere and pointed down a dirt road to the Four Corners monument. He found it; a square cement block with an emblem for each state on each of its four sides. He pondered it awhile, straddled his feet and hands into four states, then moved on. He walked for what seemed twenty miles, but was really only ten, then stopped under the last tree in sight, sloughed off his pack, and changed into his buckskin pants and shirt, which the Steamroller had gotten cleaned for him. He thought it more appropriate for entering into Native American territory.

He trudged on until dark, along the road he figured to be Highway 666, which Al had mentioned. He encountered no vehicles, houses, or humans. He cut off into the wilderness and in the dark found an overhang of sandstone in a shallow gully. It would have to be his shelter for the night. The temperature dropped to cold, then very cold. He put on his blue city jacket Steamroller had bought him, over his buckskins, and rolled up in his bedroll. A coyote yipped in the distance, and was answered by others, which proved to him he was in the wilderness. He was lonely, so lonely, in the desolate land, and thought of crying, but tears refused to come. Finally, sleep came.

The Seeker awakened with the first rays of the sun finding him, but he stayed in his bedroll until the earth and air warmed.

His body was stiff from the cold and hard ground. He opened a can of beans, ate them cold, and washed them down with several swallows of cold water from his canteen, then re-packed, and wearily started his trek again.

He walked for two more days and nights, and slept in the fickle desert that was cold at night, hot during the day, and sent whirlwinds and flying sand that needled his skin and at times threatened to blind him. On the third morning, he awakened to find a jackrabbit snuggled against him for warmth. He walked on, asking himself what he was doing out in this wilderness. The answer came. What else could he do? He had christened himself the Seeker and Elijah had directed him to seek after his Indian friends, then other necessary events would follow in his life.

He looked up from his thoughts at the vast expanse before him. Was that a city he saw in the distance, shining golden in the sun? He quickened his pace. As he drew closer, it did appear to be a city, a very different kind. One turned to stone, red and gold in the sun, with skyscrapers, cathedrals, spires, palaces, sandstone, slate, and rock. Magnificent structures created from stone in many architectural designs. He knew he had never seen this before, even in his other forgotten life. Time must have left this place. Space around it stretched forever.

The boy turned in circles to take it all in. Behind him a trail of red dust rose. A horse-drawn wagon. It came toward him and stopped. A brown skinned man sat in the driver's seat, a wide brimmed hat perched on his head. Two women sat in the buckboard dressed in bright colored skirts and blouses, all with long, black braids held together with beaded ties. Native Americans! Did they know Elijah? They had heard of him, but he would have to go to a place called Canyon de Chelley; that is where the people live that know him. They would give him a ride closer to that place. He climbed in the ancient wagon with the two women.

Two hours later, they dropped him off. They were bound for another direction. They pointed the path he should follow and told him he really needed a horse, but if he was a good walker and patient, he might make it.

It was not until the dust settled from the wheels of their wagon and they had disappeared in the distance, that he suddenly realized he had spoken to and understood them in their native language, Navajo. He found this interesting, but somehow he was not surprised. So many unexplained things had happened to him. And the Prophet Elijah had said he had been blessed with power in language.

Another night and his food and water were about gone. His stomach rumbled. How good one of Aunt Ellie and Uncle Elmer's steaks would taste. But his weariness was greater than his hunger. He was asleep as soon as he crawled into his bedroll.

He walked, his body numb. The sun was hot, waves of heat rose from the hot sand. He was discouraged. He came to a large chunk of sandstone, dropped his pack, which had become heavier with each mile and footstep, and stretched out. He ate his last peanut candy bar and drank three swallows of his water. Only a few ounces left. Was this his end? Was the Seeker to perish alone in the desert?

He turned on his sandstone seat and struggled to sit up. He would read his Bible. He took it out of his pocket. It was bent, dusty, and finger-worn. Desperately, carelessly, he opened it. There it was again. The same words in a different place. He had read it in several chapters; different prophets with the same advice. This time in Matthew 7:7: 'Ask, and it shall be given you; seek and ye shall find; knock, and it shall be opened unto you.'

He had been seeking long and hard. Now he would ask. He raised his face and arms to the sky. "Great Father of Heaven and Earth. I am Jared the Seeker. I have done all I can. I ask for your help." He lowered his arms and a butterfly landed on his nose. He crossed his eyes to see it. A swallowtail. A tiger swallowtail. His spirit guardian. He had not asked for a sign. It was wrong, he felt, to ask for a sign. Nevertheless, it had to be a sign. this was not the country nor the time for a butterfly. They stared at each other for many seconds, then the butterfly flickered up and seemed to disappear.

He contemplated this event and felt a presence near him. He turned and saw a beautiful face staring at him over a sandy knoll. He saw dark eyes and black hair tied with a red headband. It was a cocoa brown Indian girl, probably his age or a little older. She turned to run.

"Don't leave!" he shouted. "Please stay. I need help."

Hesitantly, she returned. He smiled and she came closer. "My name is Jared. I am lost," he explained. "A friend of mine sent me to this country. His name is Elijah."

At the mention of Elijah, she smiled in return. "Yes, I know him. He used to visit my people," she explained, speaking English. "My name is Rose. Come with me. My horse is tied back here. I will take you to my family."

CHAPTER
THIRTY-THREE

They were riding bareback on her buckskin colored horse. He had his arms around her waist. She did not appear frightened or embarrassed. They suddenly left the barren desert and entered a cool canyon. Cliffs rose steep and high on both sides. A creek ran down the center, lush green lining its banks. He thought to himself, A place of refuge. I feel peacefulness. "How beautiful," Jared observed, the first words either of them had spoken since their meeting.

"Canyon de Chelley," she answered. "It is a sacred place to my people. The spirits, the ancestors often speak to us here."

They rounded an out-cropping of rock and a small shack, or hogan, appeared with a garden behind it. A huge cottonwood tree provided shade. Children played nearby. A fire burned in front of the hogan, while a large, metal pot hung from a stick on crossbars over the flames. Heavenly odors filled the air.

Rose jumped from her horse, saying, "This is the hogan of my family. Come and help me feed and water the horses." Then she added, smiling coyly, "Perhaps then we might feed and water you! My family will want to meet you because the one called Elijah sent you here." His stomach cried out for food and water, but he had learned his first lesson in horse care. Horses are very important to the Navajo. You take care of them, and they will take good care of you.

Jared left his pack with the horses and staggered behind Rose toward the hogan. A tall, lean Indian man with skin like leather and tree bark stood at the door. He looked as solid as an oak limb.

His faded jeans were tight like an outer skin and barely fit over well-worn cowboy boots with pointed toes. His hair was arranged in the traditional Navajo chignon and tied with a blue scarf.

"Father, I found this boy in the desert, " Rose said. "He says Elijah sent him here. He is tired and plenty hungry."

"What are you called?"

"I have named myself Jared the Seeker. I will tell you my story later."

"If this is true that Elijah sent you, then you shall be a member of our family as long as you wish to stay. We will call you Seeker. You may call me Wolf. Come inside and meet your new family."

It was dim inside the hogan and it took awhile for Jared's eyes to adjust after the bright sunlight. Gradually, he was able to focus on a plump woman kneeling over some bowls. An old silver haired man with a hand-woven red, black, and yellow blanket around his shoulders sat in a far corner. The children, who had been playing outside, crowded into the hogan, curious to see the newcomer.

"This fine woman preparing food is the mother of these seven children," said Wolf. "She is called Bird Lady. "She nodded at the new boy. "And this wonderful gentleman sitting over here is our grandfather. He is blind, but sees more with his spiritual eyes than the rest of us all together. He is known as Te Maunga, The Mountain. He shares his wisdom with us. You can learn much from him, if you will listen. You have met Rose. And this boy, who is almost as tall as yourself, we call him Chipmunk. These other smaller ones you will get to know as time passes.

"Now," continued Wolf. "Bird Lady will give you a cold drink, then you can go down and wash yourself in the stream. If your belly can hold off for an hour, you shall have some food with us. Afterward, you can tell us your story.

The food was delicious, with hot stew, squash, beans on the side, and plenty of Navajo fry bread, which he learned to love better than desert. He told his story. All of it, even the part about waking up in a pine tree. When he took off his shirt and showed them his scars from the bear attack, all the children's eyes became big as quarters.

Finally, they all rolled out their sleeping mats and blankets and stretched out in the one room hogan with a dirt floor. All eleven of them, head to head, head to toe, toe to toe, back to back. The Seeker felt at home. He slept. And slept and slept. When he finally awoke, he did not know whether it was day or night, until a voice told him.

"I have saved you two meals and another one is about ready," said Bird Lady. "You have a lot of eating to catch up on," she said, chuckling. The grandfather laughed lowly in back of him.

"What time is it?"

"We don't keep track of time around here, but you have slept a night and a day. The sun is going down again."

"I'm sorry. Oh, I'm real sorry, being so lazy," Jared apologized.

"No need to apologize. You are not lazy, just tired. We will get plenty of work for you later." She chuckled again.

A happy person, he thought. One who enjoys life.

CHAPTER THIRTY-FOUR

He took his turn with the chores, feeding and watering the horses, hoeing the garden where there was corn, gourds, beans, and squash and gathering firewood, carrying water from the stream. And one of his pleasures; playing with the children. He had learned all their names, ages, and individual personalities. They seemed to adore him. "Seeker, tell us another story. Seeker, carry me on your shoulders. It's my turn next," they pleaded.

He also spent long, lazy days in the sun tending the sheep and goats, mostly with Rose and Chipmunk and sometimes with the younger kids. He became very fond of lithe, lovely Rose, with her high cheek bones, heavily lashed black eyes and full, pink mouth. She stirred feelings in him he had never felt before.

They sat in the shade of an outcropping of sandstone. Chipmunk was on the far side of the sheep. "Tell me," he asked. "How did you get your name, Rose?"

She studied him for awhile. He had learned that Navajos were rather silent people, never in a hurry to talk. Finally, she said, "I think you should ask my father that question. He is the one who named me. I have heard the story many times, but he should be the one to tell it. It is special to him. It has meaning in the lives of my father and mother."

"I will. I will ask Wolf to tell me sometime." He looked shyly at her. "I like your family. I like them very much." He hesitated, hoping he would not overstep certain limits, but added, "And I like you most of all."

She steered away from his last statement, and replied, "It is your family, also. Like Wolf said to you, we are your family now as long as you wish to stay."

Both gazed out over the vast desert around them. It was summer and the days had become very hot. She turned to him after a long silence. "I do not know of your former life because you do not remember it. Perhaps our worlds are different. But if you stay with us for awhile you will begin to understand that we are people who are close to this earth. You will begin to understand that the soil beneath our feet, from a grain of sand to the highest red mountains of many shapes that you see – all is sacred. Especially sacred to us is the Canyon de Chelley. It is a place of the gods where the ancestors speak to us. When you learn this; when you feel it in your heart, then you will understand us and be one of us."

Although he could not remember his past, he knew he had never seen mountains like the ones Elijah lived in, nor the red buttes, mesas, and spires here. He had never seen such limitless space, such vast skies, never been on a horse before, and never before experienced this freedom, this peace within. Some things you just know without proof.

"Did you know Elijah well?" he asked.

"I remember him, but I did not know him well. I was just a child. He used to come every summer, then he stopped. He would read to us from the books he brought with him. I liked to listen to him read." She thought for a moment, then said, "My father, mother, and our grandfather knew him well. They will want to hear you tell about him."

The day was closing. They headed back to the hogan. Seeker rode behind Chipmunk on his horse. They followed Rose on hers. He did not want his feelings for Rose to appear too obvious, so he rode with the talkative, chubby, little brown eyed boy who had become his shadow, wanting to hear more of his adventures, especially about his American football friend Steamroller. Strangely, he was even quiet as they rode along in silence.

Seeker pondered Rose's remarks about the earth and this land around them in Dinetah, as the Navajos called the domain. He looked at it now with new eyes. The sun was dipping low in the west on its sky journey. He thought of it as going across the earth each day, rather than the earth revolving around the sun, though he knew differently. Its rays now only reached the tops of the sandstone spires, lighting them like candles with flames of yellow, orange, pink, and deep red down lower. Even lower upon the landscape, fingers of blues and purples stretched out into crevices, ravines, and canyons. This endless space of earth was constantly changing, never the same form one moment to the next. He began to understand a little of what Rose had said about it.

Stars appeared just as they reached the stream that wove through the now familiar canyon. Ahead, the welcome cooking fire could be seen for the evening meal. They gathered to eat in silence, all eleven of them, each night, and sat in a circle, cross legged upon the ground around the fire, the young children helping the grandfather, Te Maunga, to his usual spot.

When eating was done and dishes washed, there was talk. Guessing and word games were played. Stories, jokes, and riddles were told. Seeker had been a part of them long enough to chance a request. "Wolf, would you tell us the story of the naming of your daughter Rose?"

Wolf chuckled. "I have told it so many times, my children have memorized it. They would be bored."

"No we wouldn't, Father. It is a good story," said another.

"Alright," he replied, reluctantly. "Only because or our new son and brother, Seeker."

All settled back comfortably and quiet prevailed.

"It was hard times for Bird Lady and myself," he began. "There was a drought, famine. We had carried water to our beans and squash. Now, this stream was drying up. No work to get money to buy anything at the trading post. We were a young couple, expecting our first child. I thought I better go to Gallup in New Mexico and try to get some work to buy some store food. I went to my friend, Tom Nez, upstream a ways. He loaned me his old pickup truck, the only one in the area. He also loaned me ten dollars and put an extra can of gas in the back. Tom was a single man, who seemed rich to us. I said I would pay him back when I could, and he said not to worry.

"There weren't what you'd call roads, just dirt trails and desert mostly, but I found my way to Gallup. I asked everywhere for work. Said I'd do anything. They all said, more or less, that Indians were lazy and couldn't be trusted."

Wolf wiped the back of his hand across his mouth. Jared could tell it was difficult for him to recall those sad memories, but he swallowed some water from a tin cup and went on with his story.

"I was desperate by then and thought of going to one of them saloons for some whiskey, but luckily I had spent the ten dollars to fill the gas tank and can, and bought two cans of pork and beans and a sack of gingersnap cookies for my wife.

"I was on my way out of town to head back home, when turning a corner of this quiet little street, I spotted this beautiful flower garden in front of a little house. I pulled over and got out of the pickup and just stood staring at those flowers. I had never seen those before. An old gentleman saw me and came out of the house. "Beautiful roses, aren't they?" he said.

"I have never seen that kind before," I told him. "They are called roses?"

"Yep, roses," he said again.

"I would buy some for my wife, if I had some money," I said to him.

"Flowers aren't to buy and they aren't for sale," he stated to me. "Flowers are free like birds are free. Money shouldn't enter into talk about them. Stay right there," he said, and he went into the house and came out with a cutting tool and a skinny bottle of clear glass. "Where you from?" he asked.

"Over there in Arizona. Out in the desert country," I told him. "I came here to find work, but didn't find any."

He cut six of those roses, put them in the skinny bottle, and filled it with water from a pipe that came out of his house. Then he handed me the bottle of roses. "I cut the roses in buds before they could bloom out," he said. "If you make it back to your home fast enough and keep water in that bottle you might get the flowers to your wife."

I was so stunned by this old gentleman giving me them red roses that I almost cried. Then, as I was getting back in the truck, he came out with a sack of flour and threw it in the back. "That's to make you some bread and biscuits. Should hold you for awhile," he said and waved me off.

I was so overcome, I prayed to the gods that they would smile on that old guy forever and ever. Well, to get to the end of my story. I made it back with those roses in pretty good shape. I dropped off the pickup to Tom Nez, gave him half the flour and a can of beans, then stumbled on to our place with my load and carrying the one red rose in the skinny bottle. Bird Lady cried and cried when I gave her that rose.

"I was tired and happy that night, but had to get up early because Bird Lady said the baby was coming. There was no one else to help, so she told me what to do. I must have done everything okay because that baby came making crying so we knew it was all right. We cleaned it up to find it was a beautiful dark eyed girl. And more good luck came to us. It started to rain.

"Now most Navajos get two or three names; a sacred Navajo name, an American name, and sometimes an everyday name, like Chipmunk here. But, or course, me and my wife named our first child Rose and that is her only name, and she is the same fine girl who found you out in the desert."

Bird Lady had tears in her eye. Rose turned her head shyly away.

"That is a wonderful story, Wolf. I thank you for telling it to me," Jared said quietly.

CHAPTER THIRTY-FIVE

"The old one, Te Maunga, our grandfather wishes to visit with you, Seeker," said Wolf, mounting his horse. "He wishes to be alone with you this day, so you will be excused from your duties. Talk with him freely. And listen well to him. He is a man of wisdom. Learn from him."

Jared now felt completely at home with this Begay family; he felt like they were his family. And they accepted him as their own. He wondered again about his family from his other life. What would they think of these humble Indians he now accepted as his own?

The sun had just peeked into their canyon and began warming the land when he entered the darkened hogan. He had learned to adjust his eyes more quickly. Everything was now familiar to him. "Take the grandfather down by the steam," said Bird Lady, as she busied herself making fry bread patties. "He likes to listen to the flow of the water."

"Let me help you, grandfather," offered Jared, stooping to the left of the old man. As he put his arm around his waist to help him to his feet, Jared was shocked by the old gentleman's thin frame; just skin stretched tightly over old bones.

"Thank you, Seeker," said Te Maunga. "It is no fun being old," he said, chuckling. "Don't let anyone fool you. I hear the white Americans call them 'The Golden Years.' Not so. More like the creaking bones years." He chuckled again, then coughed several times.

Te Maunga walked like a half-open pocketknife, bent almost in half from the waist. He used a short walking stick with intricate carvings on it, which he always had at his right hand and leaned heavily upon, his loose buckskin robe dragging the ground in front. His skin was like rough tree bark, his hair to his waist and the color of summer clouds, his sightless eyes a liquid gray-white.

Jared held him tightly around the waist and carefully picked their way down to the stream where they sat on a grassy spot.

"Thank you, my son. Thank you," the old man said, gasping for breath. After he had rested, he said, "Ah, I feel the warmth of the sun. It begins to heal my brittle bones. Though my earthly eyes no longer even distinguish light nor dark, I can tell the day from the night. I can tell the seasons. I have learned to feel through my skin. I have learned to smell more with my nose, to hear more with my ears, and to taste many things with my tongue, all since my earth eyes left me."

"How long have you been blind, Grandfather?"

"It seems like forever, but my sight began to fade the year after my granddaughter Rose was born. It gradually got worse, until I could only distinguish light from dark. Them finally, all darkness. That is when my son and his wife brought me to live with them. The loss of my earth eyes has taught me to see with my spirit eyes. I will give you a secret. The physical and spirit worlds mirror each other. The Creator made the spiritual world first and it will be here after the physical world is destroyed, turned to ashes, blown away by the eternal winds.

"Now I want to learn about you, my son, you who have named yourself the Seeker. Describe for me our surroundings. What do you see in all directions around us?"

Jared began to look more keenly at their surroundings. He wanted to be, for this moment, the eyes of this old man. "Where we sit," he began, "is tender grass, bright green where the sun shines upon it, darker green where it is shaded. It slopes gradually down to the stream that runs smoothly at this spot, then bubbles swiftly over rocks farther down. Along the banks grows mint smelling plants and a few tiny, white flowers. Long strands of moss wave in the water, like the hair of a phantom princess, dark green, darker than grass.

"Behind us, Grandfather, up on the rise, is the hogan made from logs, willows, sod, and clay. As you know, it is warm when the weather is cold and cool when the weather is hot. Four chickens are pecking and scratching in front of the doorway. A large cottonwood tree grows to the upward side of it like a giant, protective hand. Behind the hogan is the garden where gourds, beans, corn, and squash are growing. It is a well-kept garden.

"On both sides of the stream, back quite a ways, steep cliffs rise, forming a canyon that stretches forever in the distance."

They listened for a long spell to the quiet, bubbling of the stream. The old man seeing in his mind what the boy had described, the boy enjoying the peacefulness of the place.

"You have let me see it well, my son. But you have forgotten one of the directions. We Navajos have six directions: North, South, East, West, Below, and Above. You have left out the Above. Tell me what is there."

The boy shielded his eyes with one hand and tilted his head back to look straight above. "I see a clear sky, no clouds. The face of the sun has not yet looked down between the cliffs on each side of us. However, its rays reach down to us so brightly that I cannot look directly into them. They are lighting the tops of these mountains into a fire of red and gold. The sky goes up, up, endlessly into what I suppose is heaven. Although it is clear, it cannot be called blue because the sun's rays transform it into a haze of silver and copper. There are two hawks circling directly above. The wind does not seem to be drifting them, so it must be a calm day, a quiet day. That is what I see above, Grandfather."

A smile was on the old man's thin lips. "You speak like a poet, Seeker. You should be one of our singers. Because you have made this day so real, I will sing one of the old songs to welcome it." He began in a high pitched, quivering voice that sounded like a mixture of chanting and singing. They had been conversing in Navajo. The old man spoke no English. The boy seemed to be born speaking the language. Occasionally, he amazed himself, but mostly

he just accepted it as a gift. Te Maunga's song lifted, floated up
between the cliffs to the sky and beyond.

> The sun comes up
> The sun rises
> All is light
> It is called day
> It is enough to say
> It is day

Neither spoke for many minutes after. It seemed that they
could hear other voices echoing the song far above them. After a
long meditation, the old man asked, "Will you bathe with me in
the spring? It is a cleaning ritual from the old days. Please help me
to sit in the water up to our waists or chests."

They stripped naked and the boy helped the old one into the
water, where they sat down. The water backed up almost to the
boy's neck. The coldness took his breath away. It did not appear to
affect the old one. They rubbed their hands briskly over their bodies and splashed on their faces. Then they got out and sat on the
grass, lifting their faces to the sun. The boy felt renewed in body
and mind as they slowly dried in the sun.

Bird Lady came, bringing them hot fry bread and steaming
herb drinks in tin cups. She handed Seeker a large wooden comb.
"When you finish eating, comb out Grandfather's hair with this,"
she said. "It's part of the old ways." She left and they ate in silence.
Then the boy began to comb the old man's long, white hair while
he smiled with pleasure.

The sun moved across the canyon to the other side, so it was
past midday. Still, they sat comfortable in one another's company,
comfortable in their silence, listening to the water, forever moving
on its journey, listening to birds and other sounds of the canyon.
Finally, Te Maunga broke the silence. "So you have been living
with Elijah," he said. "Tell me about him. We have wondered why
he no longer kept coming to us each summer."

"When I awoke in the tree, not knowing how I got there or who I was, I saw smoke from a cabin and found my way there. I was greeted at the door by a little, one eyed man who wore a patch over his other eye. This, I learned, was Elijah. His cabin is high in the mountains, which are different from these mountains. They were covered with trees; pine, cedar, juniper, and down lower quaking aspens, scrub oak, and maple.

"I learned later from Al Varner, the truck driver who brought me to your country, that Elijah lost his eye when he tried to help a drunken guy. The man stabbed him in the eye. That might have caused him great grief and drove him to his lonely life. That is probably when he stopped coming here to you people."

Te Maunga shook his head. "How sad, how very sad. What do you think of the man after living with him for many months?"

"Grandfather, I honestly still don't know what to make of him. He is a mystery. At times I thought he was a crazy fool; at other times he seemed to have wisdom beyond this world. He became friend and teacher to me." Seeker grew quiet, hesitant to ask what was in his mind.

The old man sensed his reticence and encouraged him to continue. "Go on, my boy, I feel your hesitance. We are not holding back from one another. This is a time to be open."

"Well, the thing that makes me wonder, is that there are no prophets, that they were just ancient old men in the Bible."

Te Maunga laughed for a long time then started coughing violently, until the boy became concerned. Finally, his cough subsided and he was able to resume speaking. "Why shouldn't there be prophets today? Were the Bible people better than we are, to be privileged to have prophets?"

"I've never looked at it that way, Grandfather." The he asked the question. "Do you think he was a prophet?"

The old man took on a pensive demeanor. He gazed out, as though his eyes could see and he was looking far beyond his earthly surroundings. Then he mused, as though to himself. "A prophet?" He looked at the boy, and though his eyes were unseeing, Jared felt the old man was looking into his soul. "Let me tell you a couple of things to think about," continued the old one in a stronger voice. "In my younger years, I performed duties as a medicine man. I traveled to Chinle, Ganado, Two Grey hills, Oraibi, over to Chaco Canyon, and even Third mesa. I helped to heal many people through ancient rituals. I knew how to do sand painting, did turtle shell, feather and deer antler dances. My son, Wolf, is a hand trembler. He has helped many people..."

He paused to catch his breath, for his role was teaching, and he was revealing secrets. "Was Elijah a prophet? Yes, that is what you might call him in white American language. Our people called him a shaman, which is the same. My son and myself, we possessed some limited healing powers, but this man Elijah, he held special gifts that I think came from the Grandfather of the Sky. He could bestow gifts and perform mysteries. Yes, I think he was a prophet."

"Thank you for telling me these things, Grandfather," said Jared quietly. "This relieves my mind because there were things Elijah did that mystified me. He had an owl that he said was a messenger and he hypnotized the bear with strange words and sent it waddling away after it attacked us. There were so many strange events that I often think that I dreamed them. Sometimes I am still dreaming.

The old one shifted his position on the ground and began tapping his walking stick and drawing circles in the dirt. Jared wondered if this meant their discussion was ended or maybe the old man had lost his trend of thought. But then he pointed the stick at the boy. "Listen now with your spiritual ears. I have decided to reveal to you some ancient secrets."

Te Maunga's eyes looked again as if they were gazing into another world. "Pay heed to your dreams, son" he began. "Dreams have meaning to the dreamer. They are as real as our awake lives. These are things that happen that cannot be explained, things that can only be dreamed or experienced by the one they happen to.

"If you remember on waking that you have dreamed about things at a great distance, it is because your spirit eyes have actually been there while your body was asleep. Your spirit eyes, ears, and mind do not sleep. They often travel to forbidden places and see and hear things you could not face or admit to your conscious self.

"Now think upon these things while we both meditate for a spell."

CHAPTER THIRTY-SIX

Shadows began to lengthen. The air cooled. The older ones of the family straggled in from their duties. The younger ones, playing about the hogan, became quiet. Still Seeker and Te Maunga sat by the stream. None disturbed them because the old grandfather had not signaled that the discussion was over. Finally, he decided that he and the boy had pondered enough, so he broke the silence. "Now," he said, clearing his throat, "Let's talk about you, my son, called the Seeker. Have you been on a Vision Quest? Do you know about it and its purpose?"

"Yes, Elijah sent me to a high mountain. He taught me my purpose in going."

"And did you discover your spirit guardian?"

"Yes, I did."

"Could you tell me what is your spirit guardian?"

Jared felt embarrassed again, as he had been when he told Elijah. He quietly revealed his secret. "It is butterfly, Grandfather, a tiger swallowtail butterfly."

Te Maunga's face showed surprise and pleasure. "Ah, how marvelous. You must be a special person," he exclaimed. "I have only known of one other person who was privileged to have a butterfly for a guardian. Can you think of a world without birds, bees, and butterflies? They are responsible for propagating our plants and flowers. These help to give us the air we breathe. Let me explain further." He shifted his position, licking his lips. Jared's rear end ached from sitting so long and wondered at the old man's endurance. After a coughing spell, he sipped some water, then continued.

"In the very old ways of our people, plant medicine was considered more powerful than animal medicine; this is because animals die off, but plants are immortal. They keep coming back; some plants are as old as the earth.

"I will give to you a secret. This world is unfinished and we are participating in its creation. If we plant a tree, a flower garden, or a vegetable garden, we are participating in the creation of this world. Ponder upon this for a minute," he advised.

Seeker did ponder. He had learned much of the earth and its plants and animals from Elijah the Prophet and now this Native American family, in two very different landscapes. In this land he now lived in, a land of red rock spires and endless desert, he had become familiar with its sights, sounds, and smells. He loved the smell of the sagebrush, yucca, mesquite, the glisten of ocotillo after rain, the beauty of the flowering cactus, and the shelter from the sun offered by a Joshua tree. He began to grasp Te Maunga's message.

"A butterfly! Yes, indeed...a butterfly," the old man muttered. "Elijah sent you to us for a purpose," he continued, looking up at the boy with his sightless eyes. "I think he wanted you to discover some of your roots, a connection you would not otherwise grasp. When you speak in *belagaana,* white American tongue, and when you read to us from that Shakespeare, although I do not understand that language, I perceive that you are eloquent and are from an educated family. Your white roots.

"But when you speak Navajo tongue, like you learned it as a child, a gift, you say it was bestowed upon you. But I perceive you have some Indian blood running through your veins. Might I be correct? Is your skin half brown and half white? Maybe light brown?" He chuckled at this.

"You are correct, Grandfather," replied Jared in awe. "My skin is darker than most white men, but lighter than most Indians. My native blood is from a grandmother way back many grandmothers in time." He was no longer embarrassed to tell this exceptional old man anything. "She came to me in what must have been a vision.

She came out of the clouds. She told me of herself and of my heritage. She was full blooded Cherokee."

"Ah, yes," cut in the old man eagerly. "Cherokee. They had a hard time on that Trail of Tears. Sad time. Very sad. I know about them. They had a great chief named Sequoia. He put their spoken words into crafted words that could be put on paper. He made their language so it could go on parchment. His people could then read and write their thoughts as well as speak them. A great chief and a smart people those Cherokee. Now I understand you well, my son, called Seeker.

"I want to close our talk now and tell you how much this day has pleased me. You have given me much happiness. You are a special one, who can learn easily to walk in the two world of white and Indian. As for myself, I will soon walk upon the wind into the eternal world of the spirits. I had better do it soon or the wind will just blow me away like a feather, my frame is so frail." He chuckled and coughed. "Help these old bones to get up and we had better go and eat Bird Lady's fine food I can smell. Or she might give ours away to the growing children for second helpings."

CHAPTER THIRTY-SEVEN

Te Maunga, The Mountain, walked on the wind that very night. Chipmunk found him stiff and cold when he tried to waken him the next morning for his toilet duties.

Wolf dug the hole himself, up on the rise near the big cottonwood tree, where they would place the earth body to return to the red dust from which it was made. The women wrapped him in his blankets because there was no wood to build a casket.

The word went out and spread. People came from all parts of the wide country because Te Maunga had lived countless seasons here, and he was known and loved by many. Besides his Navajo friends, some Hopi, Ute, Zuni, and a few white Americans came, which was rare for such sacred ceremonies. But they had known the old man from his visits to the trading post.

Dances and rituals were performed. Songs and chants were sung. The women wailed, like native women in many parts of the world for their dead, in a high pitched tremolo. Shaman chanted ancient words and tossed sacred cornmeal to all directions, then a handful in the grave.

Wolf, Chipmunk, Seeker, and Leonard, a boy younger than Chipmunk, lowered Te Maunga by ropes into his grave. They faced him toward the east so his face might smile at the sun as it rose each day.

Then Wolf knocked a hole in the hogan so the "chindi" or ghost of the old man could escape and find its way to the cloud people and the next world.

People brought food. A feast was prepared. The celebration of

life and death went on for three days and nights, singing, chanting, dancing, and mourning. They slept in tents or upon the
ground under the stars. Then they left as quietly as they had come.
Life for the Begay family returned to normal, and yet not normal.
An empty space was left in the hogan and in each of their hearts.
Seeker mourned the old one as if he was his true grandfather, and
in a way he was. He was his grandfather in this present life, the
only life he knew for now. He treasured the day they had spent
together, and had much to ponder of their conversation.

The younger children cried a lot for several days. They were
afraid at night because they did not understand this thing called
death. Bird Lady held them and sang them lullabies, giving them
increasing love. Wolf told them comforting tales of the cloud people
and how their grandfather would be welcomed into the next world
by his friends, who were already there, and especially by his wife,
the grandmother they had never known.

Seeker saw how wonderful a family was, and as far as he was
concerned, he was a member of a close-knit family. This was his
family.

CHAPTER
THIRTY-EIGHT

"You have become a fine horse rider," said Wolf to Seeker one day. "I have watched you learn. Rose and Chipmunk have taught you well. You still have much to learn, but I can help you become even better, I think. You should have a horse of your own. There are many wild ones out there. Tomorrow, early, we will go find some. I think that Rose might let you borrow hers for this purpose."

They rode out before sunup, Jared riding Rose's beautiful buckskin and Wolf on his Appaloosa he called Spotted Eagle. They took water, jerky, and fry bread with them because it might be a long day, even with some luck riding with them.

They rode side by side, out of the canyon into the wide desert, not speaking. The morning was brisk and chilly. The breath of the horses came out in cloud puffs. When the sun broke free, lighting up the land, Wolf pointed, saying, "There is where we will go, over in that direction. There are ravines and canyons where the horses hide. There is a water hole they drink from, also, unless it is dried up in the summer heat already. But I am sure we will find some horses over there, and if fate smiles upon us we will catch you a nice one."

Again they rode in silence, enjoying the morning, the land that stretched endlessly around them and the comforting rhythm of their horses hooves kicking up red dust. Tall sandstone spires far off broke the monotony of the desert.

"You sit straight and tall on a horse," said Wolf after they had ridden many miles. "You hold the reins well. You do not bounce up and down on the horse; you ride with his rhythm. But there is

much more you must know about being a fine horseman. We
Navajos have prided ourselves as being expert horse people for ages,
from back to the old times when we were warriors right up to now.

"You must teach your horse discipline, but teach him love.
Never abuse the horse. Only on rare occasions do you need to
shout or talk loud to a horse. Whisper to him whether riding,
standing, or approaching the horse. Whisper to him and you will
see him respond. Treat the horse as you would a friend. A horse
will become your best friend and remain so when many humans
cast you aside. But only if you love him. Most animals sense love,
just as a woman senses the love of a man. Words are often not
needed. Do you understand what I am telling you, Seeker?"

"Yes, I do, Wolf. And I thank you for the instruction."

"Good. You will learn other skills for yourself, the more you
are on a horse."

Both horses started to snort and whinny.

"Look!" shouted Wolf. "Way off ahead there. See their dust?
Our horses knew first. Looks like a fair herd of the wild ones."

They drew closer and Jared could see them clearly now. "Maybe
a dozen or more, huh, Wolf?"

"Yep. Pretty close to that number. See that big white stallion?
He's the one we want. The rest are brood mares. He will try to
steer us away from them. That looks like a V-shaped dead end
canyon off to the left. Let's try to head them there. Are you ready
for some fast and fancy riding?"

"You bet, Wolf."

"Okay, you ride to the left, I go right. Don't let him out between us. Watch my hand signals as we get closer to him."

Their horses left dust trails as they parted and sped off in
pursuit of the white stallion. He broke from the herd as Wolf said
he would. Wolf signaled Seeker to slow down a bit. He was afraid
the stallion might whirl and cut back between them. By keeping
him on a steady run they managed to steer him into the V-shaped
canyon. When he realized he was trapped, he reared and pawed
the air with his front hooves, snorting and whinnying.

Wolf was off his horse before it stopped. Rope in hand, he approached the beautiful, wild creature. It charged at Wolf, knocking him for a loop, and broke for the open mouth of the canyon, but Seeker quickly steered his horse to block its escape. He yelled, waving his arms and drove the stallion back into the V.

Wolf picked himself up, brushing off red dust and chuckling to himself. "A real fighter, aren't you, horse? I like that. Yes, I like to see that spirit in a horse." He spoke quietly as he again approached the wild, white stallion, his rope held behind his back. The horse pawed the ground, laid back his ears, flared his nostrils, and snorted.

When Wolf was within ten feet, his rope streaked out like a striking snake. It slipped over the horse's head and settled around his neck. Wolf took in the slack as the horse reared again, eyes wide with terror. "It's okay, Horse. I don't want to hurt you," he said softly. Without changing his tone of voice, "he told Seeker, "Get slowly off your horse and bring me that halter. Don't make any quick movements."

Jared walked slowly up behind Wolf and handed him the halter. "Hold this rope now," Wolf whispered. "Try to keep it tight while I see if I can get close enough to slip this on him."

He approached the powerful, snorting animal, speaking softly. He was now close enough to touch him. He quietly laid the halter on the ground, still whispering to the frightened horse. Jared could not hear what he was saying, but the soft words seemed to have the rhythm of a chant.

Suddenly, in a movement so quick Jared hardly saw it, Wolf reached up and grabbed the stallions ears, yanked his head down, and blew three times in each nostril of the horse. Then he said some more words. The animal seemed hypnotized. Wolf reached quickly down, picked up the halter, and slipped it over the snout and ears in one smooth movement. "Are you willing to try the ride of your life, Seeker?" he asked over his shoulder.

"I'll give it a try, Wolf."

"Good boy. You can let loose of the rope and I'll slip it off him. When I say go, swing up on his back, grab the rope halter, and clamp your knees…Now!"

Seeker swung himself astride the big, white stallion. It was still, perhaps five seconds, then all hell erupted. The great, white stallion bucked straight up into the air, all four hooves off the ground. He sun fished, dovetailed, then bucked high again. Jared felt himself flying through the air. He hit the ground half on his face and half on his shoulder. Bright orange sparks lit up his eyes and he lay stunned.

Wolf reached up and snatched the halter, snubbing the stallion's head down. "You okay, Seeker?" he asked, concerned.

No answer.

"You hurt bad? Let me hear you talk," he insisted.

Jared shook his head. Lots of cobwebs inside. He rose to a sitting position and found his voice. "I think I'm all right."

"Stand up, so I can tell," instructed Wolf, still fighting to control the horse. Their own horses had backed off a ways and were watching the scene, quite unconcerned.

Jared rose shakily to his feet. "Yeah, I'm okay, Wolf," he assured his companion.

"Then you have the worst ahead of you, boy. You have to get back on this critter and master him. If you don't, he will never respect you and won't ever allow himself to be your horse."

"I'll try, Wolf," Jared said, dusting himself off.

"Are you afraid?"

"yes," Jared answered honestly.

"Good, you are supposed to be. Here are the reins. Swing up while he's pretty calm." Jared swung, a sharp pain wrenching his shoulder. He switched the reins to his good hand and clamped his knees into the horse.

"Take him into that deep sand there, and let him wear himself out," Instructed Wolf. 'Then give him his head and ride him out into the prairie like the wind. He'll be ready to settle down, and you can bring him back then. I'll wait here with the horses."

The boy did as he was instructed, his head gradually clearing.

The stallion could not buck as wildly in the sand and let him have his own way. They sped off, leaving a trail of red dust flying, until they were out of Wolf's sight. The boy leaned down and talked into the stallion's ears as both felt the exhilaration of speed.

CHAPTER THIRTY-NINE

It was sometime before Wolf saw them returning at a casual trot. He was chewing some jerky and drinking from a canteen when they pulled up. "Enjoy your ride?" he asked, smiling.

"Wow!" was all Jared could manage.

Wolf got up and handed Seeker some hobbles. "Hobble him over there near our horses, but not too close. And watch his hooves. He might still try to get even with you. He is far from broke, but at least he knows you now. Couple more rides on him, this afternoon, and he might be tired enough to let you ride back to our home on him."

Jared returned and sat down wearily by Wolf in the shade of some rocks. "Have some drink and food," said the rawboned Indian, handing him the canteen and a piece of fry bread and jerky. "That there is a lot of horse for a boy your age. You did a good job. He knows you now. Just keep talking to him, so he knows your voice, too."

They chewed awhile, until Wolf asked, "How are you feeling? You took quite a hit on the ground when he threw you."

"My shoulder aches some and I guess I bruised my cheek, but I don't think I broke anything. I'm glad you made me get back on him, or I might never have done it on my own again."

"Took more courage than many bronco busters I've known. I've seen rodeo Indian and cowboy riders give it up after a toss like you had."

Jared felt warm and good inside for the compliment.

"Let's stretch out and snooze a little while, here in the shade, then we can head back," suggested Wolf.

They were entering a narrow canyon with steep walls on each

side. Jared the Seeker had worked with his horse a couple of times more out in the desert. It was still skittish, lots of fight left, but gradually he was learning to control the animal. Wolf rode behind him in case Jared needed help with his new horse, trailing Rose's horse behind him.

"Look up on those walls," said Wolf, as they rode deeper into the canyon. "See those pictures? And see those windows and door-ways looking down on us? The ancient ones lived here before us Navajos. They are called by some people the Anasazi. Nobody knows much about them, where they came from, why they left, or where they went. It is one of the mysteries."

The boy gazed up from his white horse, high up above the cliffs. "Those dark windows and doorways look like eyes and mouths of skulls howling down at us." As soon as he said that, he wished he had not. The Navajos never spoke of the "chindi," ghosts of their ancestors. They feared many of these ancient spirits. Some of them could be witches, bad spirits.

Wolf said nothing. They rode deeper into the canyon, which slanted downward gradually, the walls narrowing and closing in on them. The sky darkened. Thunder rumbled from the distance.

"We better ride fast and get out of here," said Wolf from behind. "This is not a good place to be, if the rain comes."

Jared wondered why. He thought it might provide some protection from the weather. But Wolf always knew what he was talking about, so he spurred his horse faster. More thunder rumbled a little closer. Suddenly, there was a strange, ominous roar, like the rush of a mighty wind. Wolf shouted to Jared as he looked behind and saw a wave of foaming water and sand, rolling down the canyon straight toward them, pushing cold wind in front of it. Jared frantically spurred his horse to top speed as the roar grew louder, the angry water gaining momentum. He glanced over his shoulder and saw Wolf's horse stumble and fall, throwing its rider to the ground, causing Rose's horse to fall as well.

Wolf waved Jared on, shouting, "Go, go, get out of here!" But Jared wheeled his horse around and raced back to the fallen Indian. He reached down. "Grab my hand and swing yourself up behind me!" he shouted, frantically, hoping his barely broken horse would allow it.

He was up, his arms around the boy's waist as the monstrous white stallion whinnied and took off full speed down the narrow canyon, the steed obviously more mindful of the danger of the rampaging water than the fact he carried two passengers. Water crashed over the fallen horses behind them. The stallion with its two riders broke free of the canyon and Jared turned his horse swiftly to the left, up a gradual incline, just as the waves of water crashed, bubbling, and roaring down past them. Sadly, they sat on the white horse, breathing heavily from effort and emotion, watching the water spread out over the valley below. Then came the tumbling carcasses of the dead, drowned horses in the water, which would subside, soak into the desert sand, become a trickle, and leave the animals to be picked dry of flesh by birds and beasts and soon become bleached bones.

The great stallion snorted, foam gushing from its mouth and nostrils. Seeker leaned forward, patted its neck, and softly spoke into its ear, thanking it.

They sat for a long time after the storm passed, the sun came out, and the water nearly disappeared, as though the flash flood had never occurred. Jared heard a muffled sound from Wolf and realized he was crying. He paid no attention to him out of respect.

Finally, Wolf regained his composure and spoke with much effort. "Well, we got one pretty horse and lost two pretty horses." and added, "And we are still alive." Then he did something Navajos, by nature, seldom do, he thanked the boy. "Thank you, my son, for saving my life. Now we had better get home to tell the good news and the bad news." He pointed, saying, "Head in that direction."

They rode many miles in silence, inside their thoughts, as the sun lowered itself in the western sky. Seeker's thoughts were of this man Wolf, a rough skinned, raw-boned Indian of the desert, who he had discovered also had a sensitive, feeling heart. He was a man who would miss his horses like they were part of his family. This was the man he looked to as a father in his uncertain part of his life.

"Wolf, I think this white horse should be yours, or maybe Rose's. I would feel guilty keeping him," said Seeker quietly.

"No, no, Seeker. That would not be good," he replied. "We caught him to be your horse. You have almost broken him, tamed him. He still has spirit that has not been broken. But he knows you. He is your horse. Rose will be upset, but I will try to explain to her. I know some friends over near Ganado. They have many horses. They owe me for a couple of things, or I can bargain with them to exchange maybe for some of Bird Lady and Rose's fine rings and blankets they have made. We will ride over there and get us more horses."

They rode up to the hogan as the sun dropped behind the cliffs, the moon rising in the other part of the sky.

CHAPTER FORTY

The family ran to greet them as they wearily dismounted from the white horse. "Where are the other horses?" they asked in unison.

"They are gone," stated Wolf, sadly. "We were in a flash flood."

"Gone! Gone!" shouted Rose. "You mean they are dead?"

"Yes."

"Rose's dark eyes flashed in anger and tears. She exploded in rage. She charged at Jared, beating him with her fists and screaming at him. "You promised to take good care of my horse," she sobbed. "You promised and now he is gone. Dead. You killed my horse! How could you let him die?"

Jared stood helplessly as she beat him with her stinging fists. Gently, Wolf pulled her away and hugged her to him as she sobbed convulsively against his chest. "Rose, my lovely Rose," he soothed. "It could not be helped. It was no one's fault. You should be happy to have your old father back here, holding you. I was almost swept away with the horses. Seeker saved me. I owe my life to him. Think about it, and try to forgive us both." She backed away, and sat on a sandstone rock to cry. She would miss her faithful horse.

Seeker and Wolf ate little of their supper, picking and shoving the food around in their bowls, heads down in grief and heavy sorrow for Rose and the gallant horses. That night, Jared laid back to back with Rose in the darkness of the hogan, listening to the even breathing of the children and Rose's muffled sobs. He ached all over form his tumble from the horse, but ached more inside for the lost horses and the sorrow that Rose felt. His own cheeks were wet. He wanted to wipe them away with the back of his hand, but didn't dare move so feigned sleep and thought of the vacant spot in the far corner of the hogan where Te Maunga, The Mountain, the wise old grandfather had slept just a few nights ago. He pondered many of the things the old man had said to him on the last day he had spent with him. The old man had known he was going to die, to walk on the wind, as he called it.

Jared the Seeker pondered his own life and wondered if death might be better than his mixed up life. This was one of those lonely nights for him, when he felt so forlorn that he was hollow inside. The emptiness would turn into a wrenching pain, far worse than any physical pain he had known. It was a pain of the heart. He had felt it many times.

But the old grandfather Mountain had told him how precious life is and how short. The old one was anxious to leave his life, but only because he had lived a life of full adventure and excitement, and was eager to see his wife and friends in the next world. That was how he had looked upon each day. Even in his blindness, each day was a new adventure to him. And the greatest adventure was when he could walk on the wind into the unknown.

What was to become of himself, who he had christened Jared the Seeker? And if he did find his other self, could he ever return to his old life fully and be the person he used to be after all he had experienced in this, his forgetting life? Then he remembered that Elijah the Prophet had hinted that here among these Native American he would find his old self, and he seriously questioned, for the first time, if he really wanted to.

CHAPTER FORTY-ONE

Wolf paced restlessly for three days after the loss of the animals before he announced, "We will go get us some horses. I have some cousins of the *To Dik'ooshi ii*, Salt Water Clan over toward Shiprock. I have decided that is where we will go first. If no luck there, we can try Ganado people, Chinle, lots of people who have horses."

It was the fourth day as the sun rose that Seeker, Chipmunk, and Wolf were getting things ready to leave. Chipmunk chattered his excitement incessantly, until Wolf said, "My son, we must work now, not talk. Much is to be done."

They would use saddles for such a long journey. Wolf borrowed a horse and saddle from a friend down the canyon. Seeker and Chipmunk had old worn saddles that had belonged to the Begays for years. Seeker's white stallion, which he had named Flash because he had saved them from the flash flood, had never had a saddle on him. Jared tried many times the previous day to get one on him. The horse fought viciously, until finally Jared sweet talked the steed into standing still long enough to get it on and the cinch tightened so that he succeeded in a short ride with saddle.

This morning, he had trouble again, but finally succeeded in saddling him. Wolf had taught him a secret Navajo song, passed down from the old horsemen. Jared chanted it softly as he approached the horse. It mesmerized the great stallion, almost seemed to enchant him temporarily.

Bird Lady had prepared them each a bedroll with dried meat, fruit, nuts, and precious water. Wolf knew where many water holes and creeks were located, but some could have dried up this late in the summer.

The three riders mounted. Wolf gave instructions to his family, who had gathered to see them off. "You young ones will have to work harder to take care of the sheep, goats, our garden, and whatever needs to be done. You are to obey your mother and Rose in their instructions. Do you understand?"

"Yes, Father," they answered dutifully in unison.

The riders made good time out on the open plains. Wolf rode ahead, leading the way. Chipmunk chattered at Seeker with constant questions as they followed. Seeker marveled at what a good horseman Chipmunk was for a boy of twelve years. Chipmunk wanted to know all about the American game of football, especially about Steamroller, Seeker's football player friend. Chipmunk had not had the opportunity for much schooling, such as Rose and some of the younger ones. He had always been doing man's work, helping his father, and had little exposure to white men's world. Maybe someday he could see a football game. Maybe someday he could go to the school regularly and learn reading, writing, and talking like white kids and learn of far off countries. Maybe.

As they rode, Jared tried to listen to Chipmunk's chatter and answer his questions as best he could. He also tried to think. He had so much to think about. He thought about the man riding in front of them. Wolf. The name fit him; a loner or leader of the pack. He sat tall and straight on the horse in faded jeans, worn boots, and plaid shirt. He wore a black reservation hate with wide, straight brim, crown uncreased. It had belonged to Grandfather Te Maunga, Now it was a keepsake, a momento that he would probably wear until he went to the grave himself. He was tough as the desert that had always been his home, his roots as deep in this earth as the cactus, sagebrush, and Joshua trees that shared it.

And yet Wolf was gentle inside, with a heart formed of love. He had taken Seeker into his home and made him part of his family. No questions asked. No restrictions. He had the same duties and freedoms as the family members. There was no time limit, no deadline was placed on his stay. Forever, he supposed, if he wanted.

Again, that brought to his mind his other self, the forgotten self, and his other family. What would they think of this native family, their humble hogan with its dirt floor, their food, their daily way of life? When he awoke in the pine tree he had been wearing nice clothes, expensive city clothes. So he must have been a member of a well-to-do family; a city kid, like the prophet had always chided him about. Probably a rich, spoiled kid. Would he ever know for sure?

Wolf's words floated back on the evening breeze and returned him to the present. 'We better stop here and stay for the night before it is too dark to see. We can tether our horses to that sturdy bush over there. Better hobble Flash a ways off from the others, Seeker. He is still a bit skittish and might hear the call of the wild in the night. There is a nice flat place here, where we can spread our bedrolls and have a bite of grub before we sleep.'

Jared laid on his back, watching a sky full of stars and listening to the night sounds, which were totally different than day sounds. They were more distinct, lonelier.

Something slithered up on his chest! The hair tingled on the back of his neck. Terror made his heart pound. He was staring into the yellow eyes of a large heavy rattlesnake! Its black, forked, feeling tongue flicked in and out, inches from his nose. He willed himself not to move, sweat dripping off his temples to his ears. He knew what this snake could do, the memory now fresh in his brain. He hardly breathed. But his heart continued to beat so hard in his chest he was afraid it would alarm this cold-blooded reptile. It did not rattle, so evidently it did not feel distress or threatened. Soon it determined that it had found a soft, warm spot, and curled up on Jared's chest to sleep.

He laid like a stiff board, willing himself to relax, breathe evenly. He flashed back to the day he was bitten by the big rattler near the stream by Elijah's cabin. It played even more vividly in his mind. He lived through the terror of it all again. The huge diamond back had attached itself to his wrist, its fangs embedded in his flesh. Elijah had cracked it like a bull whip, killing it instantly. The excruciating pain had moved up his arm. Elijah had cut the fang marks and sucked out as much poison as he could. The fever had burned through his body, then delirium and waking up to find the old prophet had nursed him through the crisis. The scenes played over and over in his mind.

Jared could not recall going to sleep, but he did remember programming himself not to move. He awoke with a start, eyes wide. The snake was gone! He groaned with relief and rolled on his side. Wolf was saddling his horse. He had laid out a breakfast of hard bread, fruit, and nuts. He turned, his face deadpan. ""How did you and the snake sleep last night?"

"You knew that rattler was on me?"

"Yep."

"Why didn't you get it off me? I was scared stiff," said Seeker as a shiver ran through him.

"If I had tried to move him, he might have struck you. I just hoped you knew he was there so you wouldn't roll over, or there would have been some trouble."

Chipmunk was wide awake now. "You mean a snake slept on you, Seeker?" he asked, incredulously.

"He sure did, Chipmunk, and I don't think I've been that scared in a long, long while."

"Gollee!" exclaimed the Navajo boy. "I think I would have just plain died!"

"Get yourself some of that food there," said Wolf to get their minds settle down. "Then get saddled up. We got a lot of riding to do. And take a look way off yonder. That is *Dibe Nstaa,* Navaj sacred mountain for the north. That is a good sign for us to see. I didn't notice it last night. Too dark then."

CHAPTER FORTY-TWO

Several days later, the kids spotted them way out as they came riding back to the familiar canyon. They ran out to meet them. The riders each reached down to swing a child upon the horse with them. Four new horses trailed behind them on a long rope looped around each of their necks. There was a paint, a buckskin, a sorrel, and a black with white stockings and a white star on his forehead. Wolf seemed to favor it, but said nothing yet.

The sun was straight up in the sky when they rode up to the hogan. Bird Lady came out shielding her eyes from the brightness, while Rose and two other children followed.

"Those look like pretty fine horses," said Bird Lady.

"I think they are," replied Wolf proudly. "We got them way over near Shiprock from *To Dik' oozhi ii,* your Salt Water Clan people. Also some *To Dich;ii;nil,* Bitter Water Clan. Those are fine people."

"Yes, those are good people," agreed Bird Lady.

"They let us have these four. Said they owed me for helping them out one time. Perhaps I could take them one of your fine blankets to make up the difference?"

Bird Lady nodded her consent.

We three agreed that Rose should have first choice of these horses. I see that she has already made up her mind," he concluded.

Rose was stroking the head of the buckskin as it nuzzled up to her. "It is a twin to your horse, my daughter," said Wolf, smiling at her as he dismounted. "Or maybe it is the same horse, come back from the other world because it missed you. I can't tell the difference between them."

"Thank you, Father. Thank you so much," said Rose, tears glistening in her eyes.

Wolf turned to Chipmunk. "Chipmunk, you and Seeker put the horses in the corral. We will have to mend it and make it sturdier, now that we are rich with horses." He turned to his wife. 'Bird Lady, you have three pretty hungry guys here...and tired," he added. "Sleep should be welcome tonight. Seeker didn't sleep much after that snake slept with him. He kept worrying that it would follow him and want to sleep with him every night." Wolf and Chipmunk laughed, while Jared grinned and looked sheepish.

That night in the darkness of the hogan, just as he was about to drift off into the world of sleep, Jared felt Rose's hand grope for his, then put her cheek against it, whispering, "I'm sorry I was angry with you." He squeezed her hand back in answer.

CHAPTER FORTY-THREE

The sheep shearing sheds were about a mile and a half from the Begay hogan. The sheds, sheep, and work were shared by several families. Men and many of the older boys began to gather, tethering their horses to hitching posts and letting some loose to graze. The women and younger children would bring food out later in wagons. Several large milk cans of water were lined up outside the sheds.

Seeker was eager to learn shearing. It looked so easy, the way some of the men smoothly clipped the wool with their hand shears. A couple of older men saw his interest. "Want to give it a try, Seeker?" one asked.

"I sure do," he replied eagerly.

They held a sheep for him and handed him the shears. "Don't dig them into the wool," instructed one. "Let them glide smoothly through the wool while you shear."

He went at the task seriously, but soon nicked the sheep. It flinched. "Sorry, sheep," he exclaimed. A few seconds later, he nicked it again and felt terrible.

"You need to observe some more, my boy," said one of the older men, "or you will have all the sheep wounded and angry with you." Several shearers laughed.

"It's harder than it looks," Jared observed, embarrassed.

"Tell you what," said the instructor, "you stick close to Chipmunk. Help him hold his sheep and watch closely. He is one of our best younger shearers. We'll let you try shearing one or two sheep each day, until you can do it without nicking. Okay with you?"

"Yes, I'll try my best to learn."

He tried hard, but each day had to say, "Sorry, sheep," several times. Each night, Wolf and Chipmunk gave him tips on how to hold the shears and moved them quickly, surely, while clipping. His hands and arms became strong, his fingers and palms turned to blisters and callouses from the shears. Finally, one day, he sheared his first sheep smoothly, without a nick. He felt good.

On the ride back that night, Wolf asked him, "Well, what do you think?"

"I think it's the hardest work in the world, but it makes food taste wonderful and I sleep better at night. It makes me feel good...like the work is its own reward."

Wolf smiled. "You are learning."

Another day of shearing. About mid-morning, Seeker took his break. He wiped the sweat from his forehead with the back of his hand and arm, stretched his tired muscles, and arched his back. He walked around to the back of the shed to the water can. A stranger was getting off his horse a short distance away; at least it was a stranger to him. He was a stocky, muscular Indian, with long, unkempt hair, dirty, torn jeans, naked above the waist and his arms were long, his hands huge and thick. He was in his late teens. He came straight toward Jared, staggering, mumbling as he walked.

"Are you the one known as Seeker?" he asked angrily in Navajo when he was a few yards away.

"Yes, that's me," Jared replied in the native tongue. "And who might you be?"

He was now standing close to Jared and he smelled of whiskey. "I am called Chico." he answered, defiantly, his body weaving back and forth.

"What can I do for you, Chico?" Jared questioned, innocently.

"You can stay away from my women, white boy."

"What do you mean?"

"You know what I mean. Stay away from Rose Begay. She is my woman." He insisted, his closed fist against his chest for emphasis, He swayed on his feet, eyes out of focus.

"I live with her family. She is my sister. They count me as one of them. How am I to stay away from her? She has not spoken of you," Jared continued in Navajo. "And I am not about to take orders from you," he finished.

"You think you are pretty superior," Chico snarled in Jared's face, "don't you white boy? Riding on your white horse, speaking our language. Well, I have seen you at gatherings. The way you look at her; it is not as one looks at his sister. You stay away from her, or I will make you sorry."

Jared grew angry at the intruder. "I am not afraid of your threats, Chico!" At that moment, he remembered what Steamroller had taught him about the art of self-defense. "Rose would never take a drunk like you," he stated as he drew back his head to avoid Chico's whiskey breath.

Without warning, Chico's right fist came up and smashed into Seeker's left eye. The blow knocked Jared off his feet and onto his back in the dust. A gash opened up across his eyebrow, oozing dark blood. He shook his head to clear it and rose slowly to his feet like a tiger about to attack. "Okay, Chico," he said slowly, through gritted teeth, the rage of wolves in both of them, "now I know what to expect from you. Let's see how tough you are."

At that moment, Chico rushed at him. Seeker stepped aside just enough to bring his knee hard into the raging Indian's crotch. He doubled over in pain, holding himself. Jared grabbed the Indian's hair in one hand, while the other fist smashed once, twice, three times into Chico's face. The stranger's nose spurted blood as he slumped to the ground, beaten. He spat, sputtered, as he sat in a stupor. But gradually, he regained full consciousness and slowly got to his feet. Jared did not see where it came from, but a long knife suddenly flashed in Chico's hand. He thrust at Jared, who jumped back, the blade narrowly missing his stomach. It would have gutted him.

A boot came out of nowhere and expertly kicked the knife from Chico's hand, sending it in an arc and flashing in the bright sun, only to land worthlessly in the dust some feet away. Wolf grabbed the stocky, drunken Indian boy by the throat, lifted him off the ground, and slammed him into a nearby shed wall. Then he picked him up again, and shook him, saying through gritted teeth, "I do not approve of weapons. I do not like fighting. But when weapons appear, then I must intervene. You are a no good drunken Indian, Chico. I would never allow my children to be with you. If you ever cross the path of my family again, you will deal with the Wolf! Do you understand?" and he released the now compliant intruder.

Chico was gasping for air.

"Do you understand?" Wolf repeated, again stepping menacingly toward the beaten boy.

"Yes," he squeaked.

"Say it again," Wolf commanded.

"Yes, yes, I understand," Chico agreed, crawdadding backward, away from this angry father.

"Good! Now get your drunken body out of here."

Chico staggered off toward his horse, while Jared stood silently to the side, watching. "Thank you, Wolf," he said. "But I think I could have taken care of him."

"I, also, think you could have, my boy, but I do not like unfair advantages with weapons." And he added, "I do not like drunks, especially drunken Indians." He turned to Seeker, lifting his chin in his calloused hand. "Let me look at that eye. Oooh, bad!" he exclaimed, squinting into Jared's face. " It has puffed up like a chicken egg, and you have a deep cut over it. I will ride with you back to our home to get you fixed up.

CHAPTER FORTY-FOUR

It was good that Wolf rode with Jared. He vomited twice and once almost fell off his horse. They stopped halfway back to the hogan and Wolf helped Seeker off his horse. "Here, lie down in the shade of these rocks. Lift your knees up. I think you got what is called a concussion. Bird Lady can help fix up your eye, but then you will need several days rest."

Wolf lay on his back, also, and put his hat over his eyes. "We have been working hard. I could use some rest, also."

They lay quietly for several minutes, until Jared's head began to clear and he felt a little better. "You know, Wolf, all the things that have happened to me since I woke up in the mountains, it's like I am in a dream and I will wake up sometime."

"I think you will wake up," said Wolf, rising up on one elbow. "But maybe you will wish you were back in the dream."

"Maybe so. Others have said the same thing. But I have to know for myself, know the reality from the dream"

"Our grandfather, Te Maunga, used to tell us that there are many worlds we might visit besides reality. He said there are dreams, visions, imagination, memory, and many others I can't recall. He said there is a world between reality and dream, and if we are blessed enough to visit that world we can see into both those worlds and even beyond the veil into the next world beyond death," Wolf added reverently. "I think he saw into that world before he died."

"He was a wise man," Seeker agreed. He shared much with me on our visit the day before he died. He taught me many truths. He gave me a lot to think about."

"Yes, I have been thinking about many things, too. Those books you read to us, the Bible and Shakespeare. There is a lot of

wisdom in them. I am an old fashioned Navajo. I never had learning from books. My family lives in the old ways mostly. Many of
our people live in trailers; government houses, shop in stores, drive
cars and trucks." He paused to gather his thoughts. "I like our old
ways," he continued. "I find peace in them. But I know that my
children must have book learning. I think when school starts again
soon that I will send Chipmunk to school with them. He is a good
obedient boy. He needs to have more opportunity; needs to make
choices for himself."

Wolf sat up. "You feel okay to get on your horse? That animal
has become very fond of you. You have trained him well." He
laughed, and added, "And he has trained you well, also. You work
well together in mind and body."

"Yes, I'm okay. I can make it now."

Wolf delivered him to the care of Bird Lady and Rose. He
explained what happened and left to return to the shearing sheds.
The little kids stared at Jared's left eye and bloody face in horror,
then turned and ran away. Bird Lady began preparing some medicine while Rose dabbed tenderly at his eye with a soft cloth as he
sat upon the ground in front of the hogan. "And this terrible thing
happened because of me," Rose said, then kissed him on the lips.
Somehow he knew he had never been kissed before in his forgotten
life. And he also knew he would remember this kiss forever.

His eye gradually healed, though he had double vision for
some time. He spent long, happy days herding sheep and goats
with Chipmunk, Rose, and a couple of the younger boys. They
also had time to explore many of the canyons, mesas. And desert
country. Though he nor Rose ever mentioned the kiss, there was
now a bond between them that their exchanged glances made stronger than words could ever express.

Then, one evening, around the fire, Wolf announced, "It is
time for *yeibichai*. We leave the day after tomorrow."

CHAPTER FORTY-FIVE

They came from all over the reservation by horse, wagon, in pickup trucks, and on foot. They came to the sacred canyon. It was time. Seeker had been taught many of the Navajo myths, legends, and sacred ceremonies. Bird Lady had told him how *Spider Woman* had taught them weaving. He had learned of the *Blessing Way*, *Enemy Way*, and *Night Chant* ceremonies. He had learned from Te Maunga about *diyin dine'* the spirit beings of holy people. But of *yeibichai* he had yet to learn.

He rode beside Wolf on their horses, while Chipmunk drove a team pulling an ancient flatbed wagon on which sat Bird Lady, Rose, and the children. Bright colors appeared before and behind them. There were traditional shirts, blouses, skirts of purple, green, orange, and red. Older men wore their hair tied in chignons or buns, with tall, black reservation hats with wide brims perched on their heads.

"This is a big one," Wolf explained to Seeker. "There will be eight days and nights of songs, prayers, chants, and ceremonies. *Yeibichai* is our most important gatherings. I think you will learn much about our people and enjoy it."

When they arrived at the encampment, Jared was astounded at its size and number of people, and more were still arriving. Wagons were everywhere. Small lean-tos were going up. Wolf, Chipmunk, and Seeker stretched out a large canvas over some poles for their shelter, while the rest of the family unloaded supplies from the wagon. An excitement could be felt in the air. That night, talking and visiting went on late. Children squirmed anxiously all night.

Nobody had to be awakened the next morning. The camp was

bussing with life. After a quick breakfast, Wolf said, "Chipmunk come with me. I will show the things being done and teach you of the *Yeibichai*.

They walked a ways to where a group of men and women were carving and decorating sticks. He picked up one to show them. "These are prayer sticks they are making," he explained. "Some are male sticks and some are female. You can tell them apart by the markings, see." He pointed out the markings to them. "When the sticks are finished they will be planted in sacred places. They are important to influencing weather and have much to do with fertility and the outcome of the harvest. The first four days are devoted to this."

"Let's move on," said Wolf, "and we can visit with our uncles, aunts, and cousins."

Seeker saw many people he had met at other gatherings and the shearing sheds. Wolf introduced him to many new people. They accepted him warmly as one of them. He heard the word *hozho* many times. With his gift of tongues, he knew it had many meanings and that it was an important concept, which blends together beauty, peace, and righteousness. In another context, to preserve *hozho*, every important activity must be accompanied with a song or chant. He would hear and see many of these as *yeibichai* progressed.

Chipmunk chattered constantly to friends and relatives and was full of questions for his father. He and Seeker were alert to everything and enjoying themselves completely.

The day slipped by rapidly and turned to evening. "Come," said Wolf. "We will go back to our camp for food and to prepare for this night of singing and dancing."

The ring of fire pushed back the darkness, filling the canyon with orange light, dancing with shadows reflected on stone walls. "Look!" said Wolf to his eager two students; Seeker and Chipmunk. "The dancers are coming already. They are called in our language, 'the group that sings while it moves.'"

"It is very exciting, Father," shouted Chipmunk.

"Yes, and it will get more exciting." The dancers moved single file into a circle of fires and people watching, singing, and chanting as they moved. "Observe their different rattles," said Wolf. "Each has its own meaning. See, there are deer hoof rattles, turtle rattles, and gourd rattles." As this group moved on, the women entered the circle. They were in a line, moving with a sliding shuffle of feet. They were dressed in the finest white-chewed buckskin dresses, beaded moccasins, and headbands. "See if you can spot Bird Lady," said Wolf.

"Seeker's eyes immediately locked on Rose and she smiled warmly at him. His heart beat in his chest like a drum. Her raven hair hung loose down her back, and was set off by a white headband. She was more beautiful than he had ever seen her. Emotions he had never felt stirred and boiled inside him.

After the night's ceremonies, they walked quietly as a family back to camp. Rose lingered behind her parents and managed to slip her hand in Seeker's. His dreams that night were of Rose dancing before him alone.

Suddenly, before Jared realized it, it was the fifth day of *yeibichai*. So much to see. So much to learn. He loved it all.

"The last four days are dedicated to sand painting," instructed Wolf to Seeker and Chipmunk, as they walked around the encampment. "They are created, then destroyed. There will be a painting for each day. Over here, is one being made by an artist and his assistant. Let's watch."

They squatted on their haunches to observe the artist.

"And it is completely done with colored sands," asked Seeker.

"That is correct. See how skillfully he lets the sand sift through his hand. The painting already exists in his mind."

"Why must something so beautiful that takes so much time, be destroyed?" asked Chipmunk.

The sand paintings are for healing purposes. They are sacred. The artist has learned his skill from his father, who learned it from his father, on back to the beginning. They can not be left to be desecrated."

Seeker had been kept so busy and his mind racing over the things he had learned and experienced that he did not want it to end. But it was suddenly the final ceremony, the most important ninth night of the *mountain chant or mountain-top-way.*

He sat on the ground with his Begay family. Other families did the same, forming a circle. On the outside of them was a larger circle formed of spruce branches piled up and known as the *dark circle of branches.* Later at night, they would be set on fire for the final dance, known as the *coral dance or firedance.*

The group that sings while it moves entered the circle, then gradually moved out. Then Wolf spoke to Seeker, Chipmunk, and the other children. "Look!" he exclaimed. "Here comes *Hastseyalti, The Talking Ancient One of the East.* He is the maternal grandfather of the *Yei.* He is *yeibichai,* the one for whom the entire ceremony is named."

He leaned closer to his eager listeners to be heard above the singing. "Observe his head mask," Wolf continued. "The hood is white buckskin topped with eagle feathers. The red fringe on the edges is horsehair and he is wearing a foxtail."

This tall god was followed by four dancers. He suddenly reached into a small basket, grabbed handfuls of sacred meal and sprinkled the dancers who immediately faced east. Jared had noticed a tall man sitting near them get up and leave. He was sure it was the man-god performing now. How magnificent he was.

"Here comes *yascelbai or Water Sprinkler,*" said Wolf excitedly. He brings us joy and laughter like he brings rain."

Jared noticed that the god was also tall. He wore a painted buckskin hood that reached to his shoulders and was trimmed by an evergreen band at the bottom and three eagle feathers on top. Down his back was a hand woven streamer of colored cloth.

"Evergreen is our symbol of eternal life," explained Wolf.

CHAPTER FORTY-SIX

Jared the Seeker sat alone in the vast desert land that at times seemed swallowed by the sky. It was so immense, so mysterious. He watched the sheep grazing around him. He watched his marvelous white horse nearby, flipping its head arrogantly, switching its tail at flies. Flash had thrown him a couple of times, but he had talked with him and mounted again. This magnificent creature had gradually submitted to him, not as slave and master, but as partners. It still had zest, spirit, and boundless energy. And he liked that in man or beast.

He leaned back lazily on an elbow and looked out at the cloudless sky. What was beyond it? A lone hawk circled above. He had learned to distinguish the flight of the eagle from that of the hawk. He wished he could soar like them.

For many days he had pondered on what he had seen and learned at *yeibichai*. These Navajo people had taken him, a *bilagaana*, white man, in as one of their own and had taught him much of their sacred ceremonies and religious rites. But then, his memory reminded him that he had Indian blood in him from his grandmother way back in time, who called herself Lavinia and appeared to him as *diyin dine'*, one f the cloud people or spirit beings. he had spoken of this to Te Maunga, who accepted it and taught him of *iina' ya' hool shho'*, which is an easing of vision, so that he might accept it himself as a truth.

Seeker had learned more of the meaningful things of life in his one day alone with the grandfather Mountain than he could learn in many years of classroom school and books. He had asked Te Maunga, "Old one of wisdom, what is to become of my life? I am a lost boy of only thirteen, fourteen, or fifteen years."

In answer, The Mountain had quoted him an ancient saying of *The People*: "*nizhonigoo biliina*, the beauty that you live with, the beauty that you live by, the beauty upon which you base your life. Use this wisdom as your guide," he had told him.

And he had thought upon Wolf's summary of *yeibichai* as they walked back to their shelter after the final night of the ceremony. He had said that sometimes men are as gods, and sometimes gods are as men. And both need the other. And Wolf had explained the broad meaning of the word *hozho*, a word he had heard much. Wolf had explained it simply as an essential harmony, which blends the concepts of beauty, peace, happiness, and righteousness. For one who called himself an uneducated man, Wolf was a master teacher. So much to think about. So much to learn. As he pondered, he saw Wolf riding toward him.

His Navajo father dismounted quickly. He seemed excited. "Hey, Seeker," he shouted happily. "How would you like to give up this boring job of watching sheep for a couple of days and do something exciting?"

"What would that exciting thing be, Wolf?"

"It is a big event. The race of our young men all over *Dinetah*. The best riders who think they have the best horses, they come from all over our land to compete. People bet on their choice; who they think will win. This is done one time each year. It is up north toward Kayenta.

"Do you think I could do it?" asked Seeker hesitantly. "I mean, do you think I am ready? Am I a good enough rider, yet?"

"Sure you are good enough. Sure you can do it. You and that horse know each other now. You can talk to one another. And that animal you call Flash is the finest I have seen in a long while."

"Okay, Wolf. If you think so, then I'll give it a go. Me and Flash will give it our best."

The whole Begay family traveled to the event, along with relatives and friends. Other families of the participants did the same. It wasn't as big an event as the past ceremony, but there were many people and the feeling was happy and festive.

As the Seeker looked around, he guessed here were almost as many horses as people. Horses had long been the strength and wealth of the Navajo, even back to the great warrior ancestor Manuelito, and before. Jared had learned of horses from Wolf and many of the cousins and uncles. They had taken an interest in him and spent time teaching him the old secrets with horses because they had seen how he liked them and how good he was with them. They taught him how to whisper to horses and listen to them in return.

The big day came. It was early morning, the sky clear, the air pure. The starting judged helped the young men line up their horses and calm them. Horses and riders were excited. Jared glanced over his shoulder and saw Rose smiling at him and it calmed him. He saw Sorrels, bays, buckskins, Appaloosa, pints, pintos, and palominos down the line. Some mustangs looked as though they had been caught like his stallion. There was a raven black with stocking feet, others with white blazes shaped like stars and diamonds on their foreheads; there were mares, fillies, old jug-heads, and swaybacks. He even spotted a couple of horses that looked like thoroughbreds or some Arabian blood, and he wondered how these poor Navajos could come up with such fine horses. But whether shaggy, beautiful, fine kept, or dumb appearing horses, each rider hoped or thought he and his horse had a chance to win. There was no fancy prize for the winner, juts fame, popularity, and hero recognition around Dinetah. No saddles were allowed; all rode bareback.

They would race two miles out to a lone sandstone spire that reached into the sky like a needle, go around it, and a judge was there to make sure they did, then the two mile stretch back to the starting line.

All eyes were on the man who would signal the start of the race. He was a tall Navajo, wearing a high crowned reservation hat. He raised his arm high. The riders and horses were tense. The arm fell and they were off! A cloud of dust obscured them from the crowd of watchers, until they were well out in the distance.

Jared the Seeker talked with Flash as they struggled to fight their way out of the herd. They were bumped several times on both sides. He saw two horses and riders fall. The boy on the thoroughbred was well out in front of the herd. Finally, Jared and Flash broke free of the bunch and began to sprint after the leader, the others spreading out behind them.

Before he realized it, the spire was just ahead. They were rounding it, still behind the leader. Now the stretch back to the starting line. Jared leaned low on Flash's neck, whispering to him. They closed the gap with the leader, then shot past. He could see the judges standing on each side of the finish line and half a mile ahead.

Then the unexpected. The white stallion's right hoof landed in a gofer hole. He stumbled and fell. Jared felt himself flying through the air.

He awakened, lying on his back, staring into a circle of brown faces looking down at him. "Where am I?" he mumbled through dust covered lips. 'What happened?"

Then the light. The revelation! "I remember," he shouted. "I remember now! I remember who I am! I am Jared Ellsworth! I live in Los Angeles, California."

PART THREE
DECISION

CHAPTER FORTY-SEVEN

"Was Flash hurt very bad, Wolf?" asked Jared, concerned.

They were riding to the nearest general store/gas station that in former times might have been called a trading post, in a pickup truck driven by a little old Navajo, so little he had to look through the steering wheel instead of over it. He was a cousin named Willy Nez. He had volunteered to drive Seeker and Wolf so that Seeker could call his home, now that he had his memory back.

"No, your horse was not hurt too bad," answered Wolf, after the truck had settled from a bump in the dirt road. "He didn't have any broken bones, just pulled some muscles and maybe a ligament. I have a nephew who can fix him up like new."

"You can give Flash to Chipmunk when I leave."

"Chipmunk will be going away to boarding school. But we will take good care of your horse." The truck bumped and jolted over several rocks and ruts and finally reached a stretch of fairly flat road. Wolf said, "You sure you want to leave us, Seeker? We would like you to stay as one of our family."

Jared hesitated thoughtfully. He liked these people. He liked his Begay family. He had never felt more free, more accepted. "I have to leave, Wolf. I don't want to, right now, but I must contact my parents and let them know I am alive. It will be a big shock to them. I have to go back to them, and who knows what the future has in store?"

"You are welcome here with us anytime, Wolf said quietly. "You are welcome to return *Ke'yah go*, back to the land."

They were silent for a long while, Jared's mind whirling wildly. The little man driving concentrated on the road, saying nothing, as dust stirred up around them.

"You were luckier than your horse. You could have been killed. We thought you were dead," said Wolf solemnly. "That jolt when you and the ground met must have jarred back your memory, huh?"

"I guess that's what did it. I woke up feeling strange, then remembered my old world, and also my new one. It was weird. Kind of like being two different people at the same time."

"That is maybe why Elijah sent you down to us. I think, perhaps, he knew this might happen. He knew things the rest of us didn't." Wolf chuckled to himself. "Your horse was ahead of the rest. It would have been an easy win for you. But that horse stumbled and you lost me ten bucks to that old man driving this truck." The little man's shoulders were shaking with laughter, as Wolf added, "That is probably why he is driving us, so he can be sure to collect from me."

All had a good laugh. "I'll pay your bet and also his gas," offered Jared. "I've got more money than I need, from my job in Denver and cash I had in my pocket when I woke up in that pine tree."

They reached the store after an hour's rough, dusty ride. Luckily. There was a phone. Jared's hands trembled as he repeated his phone number, punching the digits on the phone. It rang once, twice, three times. He had mixed feelings, hoping no one would answer and wishing they would, anticipating. Then a female voice came on the line.

Jared's lips were dry, his voice hoarse. "Mother, it's me, Jared."

He heard heavy breathing on the other end of the line. There was a long silence. Finally, "Is this some kind of sick joke?" My son Jared was killed in an airline crash over fourteen months ago."

Jared panicked. What to say? "No, don't hang up, mother. I am Jared. You are Jennifer. Dad is Stephen; he is a banker. My sisters are Elizabeth and Esther. We live in the Brentwood section of Los Angeles. Mother, are you still there?"

"But...oh, how could you be Jared? There were no survivors from that plane crash."

None knew about me, Mother. It was weird, almost a miracle, I guess. I must have been thrown free of the wreckage. I woke up in a tall pine tree. I didn't know who I was, didn't remember a thing. Amnesia. No one else knew about me, I guess. It's fantastic, I know. But it actually happened. I fell off a horse today and my memory came back." He rattled off his story so fast he had to catch his breath.

"Oh, Jared. Can it really be? My Jared. Back from the dead…everyone accepts that you are dead. Where are you?"

"I'm in the Four Corners area, the Navajo Reservation. I am with Indian friends. I've been part of their family."

"Oh, Jared. It's so unbelievable. Where can we pick you up?"

"I'll come home, Mother. I'll catch a plane from the nearest airport. I'll wire you the flight number and time as soon as I make arrangements. I have plenty of money. And don't worry. I've learned to take care of myself."

CHAPTER FORTY-EIGHT

Wolf was driving the borrowed truck. Bird Lady and the two youngest children were in the cab with him. In the back, Jared sat between Rose and Chipmunk. He felt Rose's hand cover his own. The three kids whispered and giggled. They were headed toward Gallup, New Mexico, where the Seeker could catch a plane and fly back to his former life.

Over fourteen months, his mother had said, since he had "died" in the airliner crash. The strange thing about it was that he vividly remembered both of his lives. Weren't amnesia victims supposed to forget their amnesia life when their memory returned? When they regained their memory of their "real" life? What was one's real life? What was reality? As the old Te Maunga had reasoned, wasn't life the reality of the subconscious? He felt strange, as though he was thousands of years old and had lived several lives. He would never be the same as before. Instead of being anxious and excited to return to his home, he felt like this was his home, here in this ancient desert land, here with his Indian family.

They arrived too soon at the airport. The young children began to cry and plead, "Seeker don't go. Don't leave us, we love you." They clung to his hands and legs. Bird Lady hugged him and cried like a mother whose son was leaving. Chipmunk hugged him and could not speak. Rose kissed him openly in front of her family, and said, "You will come back to us someday. I know you will come back."

Wolf solemnly shook his hand, saying, "We will miss you, Seeker my son. You will always have a place with us. *Yeha Noha*, which he knew meant "Wishes of happiness and prosperity," a fond Navajo farewell.

Then he was on the plane. It lifted him into the cloudless blue New Mexico sky as he saw his family waving far below and tears dampened his eyes and cheeks.

The hum of the engines took his thoughts back to that day, over fourteen months ago, when he had left to visit his grandfather for his summer vacation from school. He recalled the storm, the turbulence as the plane violently tossed about in the wind and rain. How he had suddenly seen the mountains and pine trees through the window. Then the screeching, tearing, shattering of metal and glass as the plane bounced, jerked, and began to break apart. Then he woke up in the pine tree and remembered nothing. His past was gone. Was there some reason for it all? Was there some meaning, some purpose why he had been the lone survivor? Or was it fate, just a cruel accident, a joke of mortality?

His thoughts made him irreverent. The fasten seat belt sign came on. The plane was descending and the flight attendant was announcing their arrival in Los Angeles.

His family saw him coming through the crowd, his skin well tanned, dressed in his buckskin pants and jacket, moccasins, pack, long hair tied in the traditonal Navajo chignon, under a black reservation hat Wolf had given him before he left. He spotted them. Dad, Stephen Ellsworth, blond, dressed immaculate in white shirt, neatly knotted tie, three piece suit, banker's uniform. His mother, Jennifer, impeccable, frilly, blue dress and white high heels, her short, dark hair in a pixy cut around her perfectly made-up olive skinned face and brown eyes, like she had stepped out of a page from Vogue Magazine. His sisters, Elizabeth, the oldest, now into young womanhood, the younger, Esther, long, blond curls, both in Sunday dresses. He hardly recognized them.

It was an awkward reunion. Dad stepped forward and formally shook his hand, "Welcome home, son. Mom hugged him, grimaced, then pushed him away, saying, "Jared, you smell terrible; a combination of smoke, sagebrush, and manure!"

"That's not a very kind greeting for your long lost son," he said with a grim smile.

"I'm sorry, Jared, but the first items on your agenda are a long, hot shower, with lots of soap and shampoo!" she said angrily. "And number two will be a clean haircut. And we will throw out those horrible clothes."

"No, Mother, these buckskins have meaning for me."

"But Jared," she argued as they left the airport, "they are so filthy. Oh, you have grown so tall." Tears came to her eyes, smearing her mascara. "You are no longer my little boy. You look like one of those savages you have been living with."

"They are not savages, Mother!" he said curtly.

His sisters stood aloof, looking at him as though he was an alien from a distant planet. He had never had a good relationship with them. The younger, Esther, did manage to put her arm around his waist.

"Let's get out to the car and on home, "said Stephen Ellsworth. "I've got to get back to the bank."

Jared quickly covered most of his story on the ride home. Elizabeth kept holding her nose, stating, "he smells terrible!"

Finally, her Dad said, "Elizabeth, please be quiet. Sometimes I think you could use a little dirt, get to know some of the dirt there in the world."

"Amen to that, Dad," agreed Jared, smiling.

There it was. The house that had entered his dreams so often when his memory was gone. The Brentwood section where only the elite lived. Wealth. Position. Power. He, Jared Ellsworth, had been pampered like other kids in this area. There were swimming pools, tennis courts, backyard barbecues, where only "important" people were invited. They wore the best clothing, best sports equipment, attended the best schools. He had it all! How different from the life he had just left behind. He could not help but make comparisons.

When he came out of the shower with a towel around his waist, his mother asked, "Are you sure that long, grimy hair is clean?" Then she gasped as she noticed the scars from the bear's claws. "Oh, Jared, how horrible! When you said a bear clawed you, I expected a few scratches."

"No, Mother, that bear meant business. He laid my arm and shoulder wide open. If it hadn't been for Elijah, the old man I was living with, I would have been a goner." He did not want to tell her how the prophet cast a spell on the animal. That would have been too much for her to swallow. "Yep, he scared the bear away, got me back to the cabin, sewed me up, cured me with herbs, and spent weeks of therapy on my arm, until I could use it again."

His mother grimaced. "And scars on your hand from the snake bite and knife. And that awful scar tissue through your eyebrow, what about that?"

He avoided explanation, and mumbled, "That was something I couldn't avoid. It just happened."

"It makes you look like a prize fighter, you know. Lots of boxers have their eyes all scarred up." She clouded up like she was about to cry. "Oh, Jared, it's just…just that you are not the same. You seem so old."

"I am NOT the same, Mother. It's true that I am older. Much older than the fourteen months I have been away. I suppose I should say I am very lucky to have survived it all."

"And waking up in a pine tree. Incredible. It sounds so incredible."

He sensed a trace of unbelief in her voice. "Yes, it's incredible," he agreed, looking into her eyes. "I still ask myself why me? Why was I the only survivor? When the plane broke up. I guess I was thrown free."

"I have hesitated to tell you, Jared, but your grandfather died two months after he heard you were gone." She looked at him rather accusingly, dark eyes sparkling, as though it had been his fault. 'Died of a broken heart, I suppose." she finished, arms crossed over her chest.

He choked as he replied, "I'm sorry, really sorry. I liked grandpa a lot."

Then her voice was back to all-business. "Your room is the

same as when you left it. Get in there and get dressed and I'll drive you down to get that hair cut respectably. I can work you in at your father's barber. Our family must convey a good image. Your father is now THE senior vice-president of the bank. Mr. Spencer, the president, is old and ailing and is soon expected to step down. Your father should be next in line to take over.

CHAPTER FORTY-NINE

She was right. His room looked the same as when he left. Nothing had changed. Except none of his clothes fit. He had grown too much. He finally found a baggy T-shirt he could get into and struggled into a pair of jeans three inches too short and he could not button the top.

"Oh, my, you have grown," his mother sighed. "We'll go downtown after the barber and get you a whole new wardrobe."

It was an awkward silence as he rode with is mother. They did not know what to say to each other.

When they arrived home with a carload of new clothes, he noticed his buckskin outfit in the garbage can. She had thrown it away. He secretly retrieved it and hid it deep in his closet. He would sneak it to the cleaners later.

Dinner in the evening at the Ellsworth house was almost a formal occasion; a ritual, stilted atmosphere. It was about the only time Stephen Ellsworth's presence was felt. He was a handsome man, tall, blond, and blue eyed. He wore a suit most of the time, even when in his study. His wife was a contrast, with her dark looks. Both girls were blonde and blue-eyed, so Jared thought his own coloring must have come through his mother's side. His Indianness. He kept thinking of his vision, or whatever it might be called; his visit with the lady from the clouds, who said she was his grandmother with several greats in front. She had called herself Lavinia and said she was Cherokee. He knew this visitation had taken place, yet he still wondered if he had imagined it all.

The usual dinner silence was broken by Stephen Ellsworth. "You look much more respectable, son. Nice haircut." Elizabeth, the oldest sister, quickly added, "And you smell much better, also, Jared."

"Thanks," he replied sarcastically. "I'm glad my cleanliness is acceptable." His mother and father exchanged quick, worried glances.

Esther, the youngest, saved everyone from this tense moment by the first of many questions. "And you actually lived with a crazy old hermit in the mountains?"

"Yep, but he wasn't crazy. He saved my life once and maybe twice. He taught me many things."

"And you lived with an NFL jock?" she continued.

"That's right."

"And you lived with Indians and slept on the ground?"

"I certainly did. They accepted me as one of their family, took me to ceremonies, and taught me some of their language." He did not want to tell them of his gift for languages. He sensed their skepticism of some of his experiences. "Wolf, the father of the Begay family, taught me how to tame and ride wild horses. I was racing with Navajo boys on my white stallion, Flash, when he fell and hit the ground hard. That was the jolt that restored my memory."

"It's hard to believe you have bee through all that," said his mother. "Just so incredible." She shook her head doubtfully.

"It does sound incredible," Jared defended himself, "but it happened and much more. I have spared you all the gruesome details," he added thoughtfully. "Yes, I have been through a lot. More than I can believe myself."

"We have plenty of time in the future to hear more of Jared's adventures," cut in his father dryly, "now let's let him enjoy his first decent meal in a long time, I presume."

All fell silent obediently, with just the tinkle of silver knives and forks on china plates. Jared sneaked glances around the spacious dining room, with its pastel blue, flowered wallpaper, lead crystal chandelier overhead, floor to ceiling windows on one end, plush, pale, blue carpet, massive mahogany dining table, sterling silver utensils, and the best china. Suddenly, it hit him. This was a dream he often had. He was in a beautiful house with these people. They treated him politely, but he felt like a stranger, like he did not belong.

As soon as he finished eating, he excused himself to go to bed. His room was the dream of many boys, with oak dresser, the ceiling to floor bookcase filled with classics, histories, and, biographies. The walk-in closet filled with enough clothes for ten kids. His own oak desk and pen set. A huge brass bed. He should be jubilant at being back home. But he felt empty, lonely. Why?

He was weary in every bone and muscle. His mind was weary. He undressed and pulled on the bottoms of his white, silk pajamas and flopped on top of his bed. But sleep would not come. The bed was too soft. He tossed restlessly. His mind was not at peace. It must have been the middle of the night before he drifted off.

His mother was shaking him. Sun streamed through the window. "Better get up, Jared, and get some clothes on. The word has spread. You are famous, a celebrity. The front yard is full of newspaper journalists and television people. They want to interview you, ask a lot of questions." She was excited.

He shook his head to clear it of sleep and get his bearings as to where he was. He rubbed his eyes, pulled on some jeans and a T-shirt, and staggered out onto the front porch into an onslaught of flashbulbs and television cameras. The questions came like a barrage. He tried to answer most of them honestly and straight forward, though he felt he had to hold back some things he knew were private and too much for these types to handle. He also had to hold back on a lot of his true feelings and give expected answers. And he certainly would not divulge his past benefactors' names and locations. It would destroy their way of life. Television cameras and reporters on Elijah's mountain or at the Begay hogan? Never!

How did he feel?

Sleepy. He wished they had let him sleep another hour or so. Laughter.

Yes, it was good to be home.

Yes, it was an incredible miracle that he should be the lone survivor of a terrible plane crash, especially being thrown into the branches of a tall pine tree.

No, he did not regret his experiences of the last fourteen months. He felt that he had learned more than he could in ten years of books and classrooms. His experiences, although difficult, had been valuable. He had learned to make decisions and be independent.

No, he did not think it unusual for an amnesia victim to remember his forgotten and present life because he had never had amnesia before.

More laughter.

The questions went on and on, until his mother said, enough, and took him into the house for breakfast.

He was on the national evening news. Newspaper stories appeared across the country.

> Boy returns from dead after fourteen months. Lone survivor of plane crash regains memory after fourteen months of seeking identity. Ghost survivor of plane crash is resurrected. Boy returns from "dead." Regains memory after fourteen months of wandering. Plane crash survivor no one knew about regains memory after fourteen months as amnesia victim. Had unbelievable Indiana Jones-type adventures. Lived with a hermit in a mountain cabin. Lived with NFL football hero. Adopted by Indian family on Navajo reservations in Arizona and New Mexico. Victim of bear attack and rattlesnake bit, etc. etc.

Most of this, the reporters had gotten from his mother. References to the hermit and Indians was too close for comfort. He wished to protect them.

Once again his life would take another drastic turn and never be the same. Constant change! The *game of life* he began to call. And he hoped he would always be a good player. He had become an overnight celebrity; the ghost boy returned from the dead.

CHAPTER FIFTY

Jennifer Ellsworth had picked up on one of the questions a reporter had asked her son: *Didn't he think it unusual for an amnesia victim to remember both his forgotten life and his life before and after his amnesia?* She had felt Jared's remarks and his behavior were quite strange since his return home. She must take him to be "checked out" physically and mentally. "Jared, I've been thinking," she began hesitantly. "Since your return, that you should have a good physical and mental examination."

"Mother! You mean go to a head shrink?" he cut in. "You think I'm kooky? That I have lost my marbles or something?"

"No, Jared, just a precaution. You have been through a terrible trauma; the plane crash, your memory loss, the strange people you have lived with. You need to be checked out thoroughly anyway, as school starts next week. It is for your own good."

"But, Mother…really…a head shrink?"

"There is no stigma anymore, dear. Lots of people have been to what you demeaningly refer to as a head shrink. I have been myself, sometime back when I was experiencing some emotional difficulty. I know a very competent psychiatrist. I will call him and make an appointment. And you can see our family physician for a physical exam."

"I can't believe it," he mumbled. "My own mother thinks I might be nuts."

She shook her head and sighed her frustration.

The family doctor pronounced Jared the best physical specimen he had examined for his age. "Top A-1 condition!" he announced to Mrs. Ellsworth. Jared smiled with satisfaction at his mother.

The head shrink might be different. He had never been to one and was filled with apprehension as the psychiatrist introduced himself. It was two days later, two days in which his anxiety mounted. His mother was able to get an appointment with this busy doctor only because of her acquaintance with him. It seemed that everyone in their elite neighborhood had to have their own "Therapist" as they called them, someone they needed to help them "sort things out" in their mixed up lives. Didn't anyone solve their own problems anymore?

Jared's fears melted as soon as the psychiatrist introduced himself. He was smaller than Jared, a frail, bald man. His faded denim-blue eyes looked out through round, wire-rimmed glasses, which he was continually pushing back up on his nose, which twitched nervously. His slight buck teeth twisted his mouth into a perpetual smile. He reminded Jared of Bugs Bunny about to chew a carrot. Jared had to bite his tongue to keep from saying, "What's up, Doc?"

But he liked the man immediately when he stuck out his hand, saying, "Hi, Jared. I'm Len Wall." Not doctor or psychiatrist Wall, but just Len, and his handshake was surprisingly firm. He turned to Mrs Ellsworth. "Jennifer, I'll be with Jared about an hour or so, so make yourself at home." He led Jared into his interview room. Jared quickly surveyed it. "Where's your couch?"

"My what?"

"Your couch. You know, where your patients stretch out and tell you their dreams and whether they step over cracks in the sidewalks...all that stuff?"

Len Wall laughed until tears filled his pale eyes, then took off his glasses and wiped his eyes with a kleenex from his desk. "Oh, those kind are psychoanalysts. I don't do that stuff." He looked the boy straight in the eyes. "Pull that big chair up to the desk. It's your couch for the next hour. I like to look people in the eyes when we talk. I've heard about you from television and newspapers. Now I want to hear your version; all of it you feel you can tell me."

Jared felt that this head shrink was different. He was honest, straightforward. He would not lie to him.

They emerged one hour later to the minute.

Jennifer Ellsworth turned to her son. "Jared, would you go wait in the car while I talk to Doctor Wall?"

Jared liked this man even more when he said, "No, no, no, Jennifer. I wish to talk with both of you together. This is about Jared, so I will talk with him, also. I have nothing to hide from him."

He led them into another room that was sparsely furnished with only a circle of six straight backed chairs. He motioned them to sit down, then took one of the chairs and straddled it backwards, facing them. "Now, Jennifer, to ease your mind. Jared is not mentally disturbed, as you might perceive that term. He has been through extreme trauma and has survived amazingly intact.

"As to your question, 'Isn't it unusual for a person who has suffered amnesia to remember both of his lives when he regains his memory?' Yes, it is unusual, but not all that uncommon. There are many known cases of individuals who clearly remember both their former lives and their amnesic period. Subsequently, it may cause such individuals to make comparisons and this may cause conflicts in their thinking. I emphasize 'may.' Jared is mature beyond his fourteen years, in mind and body, so he has, perhaps, a good chance of resolving his conflicts. But often these conflicts involve choices, which show themselves in actions, behavior, which may place stresses upon the family." He turned his attention toward Jared. "You are already making comparisons and choices, aren't you, my boy?"

"Yes. Yes, I am. But many of my choices are vetoed because I am a child and parents are adults. I have to always give in to their choices and decisions."

His mother flinched.

"That, I can acknowledge. Your readjustment to your present environment will undoubtedly be difficult," continued Doctor Len Wall. "It will be difficult for you and your family. Compromise is the key for both of you. Compromise is a difficult thing for anyone, especially for strong willed people, such as I sense both of you are." He smiled to ease the brunt of this.

Doctor Wall spent another hour with mother and son, suggesting possible future agendas for the family. Then he released them, offering to see them again, if they felt the need.

CHAPTER FIFTY-ONE

The ride home was another awkward silence between mother and son, until Jennifer Ellsworth finally brought up another touchy subject. She approached it hesitantly. "Jared, about your schooling," she began. "You have missed an entire year of school, so you will have to start in the ninth grade."

"M-o-t-h-e-r! No, not ninth grade. I'd feel like a thirty-year-old with a bunch of kids. My class, the kids I know, will be starting high school! And me sitting in a little junior high desk!? Look at my body. I've grown, developed, since I have been away."

"It's not your body I'm concerned about," stated his mother, face flushed, her voice rising. "It's your mind I am concerned about. We cannot have any dullards in our family when it comes to education…with your father in line for the presidency. And what would our neighbors think?"

Jared fought to control his anger. "Mother, I really don't care what the neighbors think or what the bankers think!"

"Well," she began smugly, "you had better start caring. Your father's bank position puts food on our table, gives us a beautiful home, nice clothing, and cars. It puts us equal with the best people."

"Best people? Hah! Big joke. And your Mercedes and Dad's Porsche…I could care less!" he gritted his teeth, angry as the bear that had clawed his limb so many months ago.

"Now listen to me, Jared," his mother insisted, screaming.

"No! You listen to me, Mother. Just listen for a minute. You keep saying that I am not the same boy I used to be. Of course, I'm not the same. I have experienced things that none of you can imagine in your wildest thoughts. I have been through things that most people should not have to go through. I have lived with people that those you refer to as the 'best people,' would not speak to. But, you know what, Mother? They are fine human beings. They treated me with kindness..."

His mother started to interrupt, but he stopped her. "I am not finished, Mother. Hear me out, then you can have at me." He swallowed, his throat dry with emotion. "I learned things during those months, things I couldn't learn from books and years sitting in a classroom. I learned to work. I held jobs. I froze in the cold and sweated in the heat. I stunk, as you people reminded me. But I felt good. I *had* to make decisions

"I made money, but I learned that money isn't the most important thing in life. In fact, I never spent a penny of the money that was in my pocket after I awoke in that pine tree. I hitch hiked and learned that money doesn't buy friendship, kindness, tolerance, or love.

"And speaking of waking up in that pine tree. Have you thought of the odds of that happening? One in a billion or one in ten billion? Me, a nobody kid being thrown clear of the wreckage. The lone survivor, while all those other people were killed."

His voice lowered. "Why me?" he asked sadly, frustrated. "Why only me? I ask myself that question every day now, Mother. And you know what? I keep thinking more and more that there has to be a reason. There has to be a purpose. There seems to be a great plan waiting for us each to discover our place, our part in that plan. I hope to discover mine.

"I did learn from a couple of books during that time: Shakespeare and that little brown Bible you gave me. I named myself from that Bible. I found my name on the flyleaf, and I read where a scripture said to 'seek and ye shall find,' so I became Jared the Seeker and I set out to find my identity; my former life, my present life, but I have not found my identity yet.

"There are things that happened to me during my search, Mother. Things that cannot be explained rationally, things that cannot always be seen, but are very real. There are things that I will never be able to speak about to you people because..." he chose his words carefully, hesitantly. "Well, because they are spiritual happenings, almost sacred."

His mother was looking at him strangely, her lovely, lipsticked mouth tight. "Are you finished?" she asked evenly, claws exposed.

"Yes."

"Jared, when we gave you that Bible, we did so because it was the thing to do, and because your father and I have never been religious. We thought it might encourage you to perhaps discover your religious nature. But little did I dream that you would become a religious nut, a fanatic!" she finished, voice rising.

Both were quiet, their breathing audibly heavy from emotional drain in the expensive car. Jared finally spoke in a near whisper, as they entered the long driveway to their home. "You don't get it, do you, Mother? You don't understand a thing I have said, do you?"

"No. Quite frankly, I don't, and I find you very exasperating. But despite your weird ramblings, you are still going to start school in the grade you missed." As an after thought, she added, "And, Jared, let me say emphatically that so long as you live in this house, you will abide by our rules."

CHAPTER FIFTY-TWO

Jared Ellsworth started his humiliating and torturous school year. He was not a happy boy. He hated school, with these spoiled, pampered rich brats. He wondered how he had ever been one of them. Ralph Barrett, his former best friend, put it plainly when he broke off their relationship. "You have become really weird, Jared. I can't hang around with you anymore, or our crowd will think I am a weirdo, too."

Good riddance, thought Jared. Some friend. But he was hurt nevertheless. It cut him deeply, and he became more and more of a loner. He hated to get up in the morning and face another day...alone. He withdrew inside of a protective shell, which none could enter.

First report card: terrible.

Second report card: worse.

Stephen Ellsworth finally brought it up at the dinner table. "Son, what happened to you? You used to be an excellent student, one I was proud of. Now I am embarrassed to discuss your grades, your schooling, at the bank."

"I know what is the matter, Father," cut in Elizabeth. She was now a senior at the high school "His instant fame has turned into ridicule," she said. "My friends ask if I am the sister of the snake-bite-kid or the bear-claw-boy. Those are some of the names they call him. It is awfully embarrassing."

Esther, now a sixth grader, chimed in, "It's the same at our school, Daddy. They call Jared awful nicknames. Most f the kids don't believe his stores he's told. They think he made them up."

His mother sat quietly, trying to concentrate on her food. She spoke to her son only as necessity demanded. In fact, she had spoken to him very little since their confrontation in the car, about his remaining back a year in school.

"I'm sorry to hear this, son. But surely you have the backbone to stand up under a little ridicule. Why should it affect your grades? And an F in phys ed class? You used to love gym. It was your favorite."

They were all looking at him. I don't like to undress in P.E. They all point and stare at my scars and whisper behind my back."

"And so you sluff? You cut classes," said his father in disgust. "Fifteen absences."

"Yes, replied Jared. "I can't expect you to understand, Dad, or you, Mother. And especially Elizabeth and Esther, with your frilly dresses and perfumes and lily white skins and mod friends of the in-crowd, like you are in a plastic bubble protecting you from any dirt or contamination. Yes, I could do the school stuff, but it seems useless crap. I should have gone on to high school, then I would have shown you what I could do as a student. But no, Mother insisted I stay back with the junior high children for the sake of appearance. In my mind, I have said to hell with school."

"You will stop such talk!" shouted his father.

"Yes, I'm sorry," said Jared, not sorry at all. "And I'm sorry to be an embarrassment to the family. Now please excuse me." He rose, left the table, and went to his room. This episode had replayed many times. He thought to himself, I can't blame them. I am the one who has changed. I am the different one. How and why was I ever a member of this family? I don't belong.

He lay on his back on the bed, hands behind his head. People had referred to his time away as his 'lost months.' He began to think of them as 'his found months.' He had found adventure, excitement, peace of mind. Could it be that he had found his true self during those months? Could that have been the person he was really mean to be?

His mind often wandered back to the cabin in the Rockies and the strange little man, who had called himself Elijah the Prophet. He had become teacher, mentor, and friend. Jared could actually smell the pine needles and wild flowers. He could hear the bubbling of the creek and taste its pure, cold water.

He could see so vividly the big, black man, Steamroller, who had taken him in at a crucial time. He could hear the laughter of the happy people at Aunt Ellie and Uncle Elmer's restaurant. He missed them.

Wolf, Bird Lady, and their Navajo family. Rose. Especially Rose. They had been like family. He thought of them now as his family. He could see the endless desert, broken ocassionally by buttes and mesas and red sandstone spires reaching their fingers into a blue sky full of golden sunshine. He could smell the yucca and mesquite and the ocotillo and sage after a rainstorm. His country. His because he had learned to know it and love it. He was torn apart by loneliness. What was he to do?

CHAPTER FIFTY-THREE

It was the last week of Jared Ellsworth's humiliating school year. He was approaching his fifteenth birthday. He was healthy, wealthy, and husky. He had kept up his physical training program the Steamroller had outlined for him. He had everything a boy of his age could dream of. But he was not happy. He could find no inner peace. In fact, he had come to the conclusion that he did not like his present life. He did not like himself in his present life. His old life, during his forgetting period…those fourteen months were happiness. They had become his remembering period. There were challenges, conditions were primitive compared with his present luxuries. He had hardly any possessions during that time and yet he had never felt such peace within himself. He had liked himself.

A question had been tugging at his mind; his heritage. He had become interested in his ancestry, who he really was. We are all made up of genes from ancestors who paved our way, gave us characteristics, our likes and dislikes, our personality, he knew. Our total selves. Not just from our parents, but from way back, and some of those genes could jump out again. He had learned this much from his school genetics and physiology. It had been slammed home to him in the visionary visit from his great-great-great grandmother, Lavinia. He would bring it up at dinner tonight.

The meal was proceeding mostly in silence, as usual, when his question hung like poison gas in the air, causing a more deathly silence. "Mother, are there any American Indians in our ancestry?"

She looked at him severely for a moment that stretched on forever. "Of course not," she stated haughtily. "There are no savages in our genealogy. None!" She looked almost fearful, stunned. "Why do you ask such a preposterous question?"

He had opened a can of worms, so he plodded on. "Do you have a great-great-great grandmother named Lavinia?"

"Her finely tweezed eyebrows rose inquisitively and in shocked expression. "Why yes, I do. How could you possibly know that, Jared?"

He lowered his eyes under her steady gaze and answered almost in a whisper. "She was an Indian. Cherokee. Look at her yellowed photo. I'm sure you must have one in your collection. You'll see. And haven't you wondered about your features? High cheek bones, darker complexion and eyes? And my dark skin, which the sun makes darker. Genes from her." It was certain he could never tell them he had met her coming out of a cloud!

His father and sisters stared at him in shock, their mouths hanging open. His mother's voice was cold, her lips curled almost into a snarl. "Lies! Bold-faced lies! There are none of those pagans in our background. Did those savages you lived with put these wild ideas into your head? Did they, Jared?"

Anger flushed his face as his voice rose. 'They are not savages, Mother. You keep calling them that and they are not. They took me in when I was lost, when I was nothing. They accepted me into their family." He was almost screaming. "Savages? They were more civilized in many ways than this phony, self-righteous family. And there was love…"

SMACK! His father had reached over and slapped him hard in the face. Jared felt the hot sting, but the whiplash on his feelings was worse.

"You will not speak to your mother with such disrespect! We have about had our fill of your silly ideas and behavior. Now get out of my sight. Go to your room!" he finished, pointing his manicured finger to the hallway to Jared's bedroom.

Tears welled in his eyes. "Gladly," he exclaimed, then stood, stumbled blindly to his room, closed the door, and flopped on his bed. He let the flood of tears come freely, until his bedcover was soaked where his head lay. He did not know how long he lay there, but he had cried himself empty. He felt hollow inside.

When he finally stood, there was darkness outside and in his mind and heart. Then, suddenly entering his mind from his forgetting life, came the prophecy pronounced upon him by Elijah the Prophet, his friend and teacher. The little man had told him that he would recover his memory and return to his family, but then he would be faced with a grave and important decision.

Yes! Perhaps he could return to his other life, his true self, where he could again see clearly with his spiritual eyes, and hear with his spiritual ears.

Without hardly any awareness he had pulled out his backpack from the closet. He retrieved his buckskin clothes from their hiding place. They were fresh and clean smelling. He put on the pants and pulled the jacket over his head. He had made a decision!

He knew he could make his way in the world now. Later, maybe, he could take a GED test for his high school diploma. Maybe study hard and get accepted to some college. Or maybe just enter the job field. He knew how to work and perform many tasks already. He could learn most any job he put his mind to and worked at it hard enough.

But for now, with luck, he might just make his way back to a little cabin in the Rockies and find a man who called himself Elijah the Prophet. He might be able to convince the Prophet to go with him to the reservation to be with Indian friends. He longed to see Wolf, Bird Lady, Chipmunk, and the kids. And Rose. Yes, especially Rose.

Joyfully, he began stuffing underwear, socks, a change of clothes into his backpack. Also, in went Shakespeare and the small leather Bible. He took the money from his dresser and stuffed it into his pocket. Money had not been that important in his other life anyway.

One last thought entered his mind. When he was old enough, he would legally change his name to Jared Seeker. He slipped his arms into his familiar pack, boosted it up onto his shoulders and tightened the straps. Silently, he crept down the hall, opened the door, and walked, free as a soaring eagle, out into the moonless, star sprinkled night.

The End

www.ingramcontent.com/pod-product-compliance
Lightning Source LLC
Chambersburg PA
CBHW011354010726

47494CB00008B/2317